OPERATION: SAHARA
WILLIAM MEIKLE

SEVERED PRESS
HOBART TASMANIA

OPERATION: SAHARA

Copyright © 2021 William Meikle

WWW.SEVEREDPRESS.COM

ISBN: 978-1-922551-88-7

-BANKS-

Captain John Banks had a headache and Wiggo was complaining again. The two events were not unrelated.

"Oh, there's plenty of sand, Cap. I think we can all agree on that. And it's warm. But it's no' much of a fucking beach, is it?"

The small airstrip below them lay on the Egypt side of the Libyan border and was also barely ten miles north of bordering with Sudan. It had been chosen as the closest point to their destination by air, or at least the closest point they were allowed access to. Banks' problems were mounting up already; after landing, the rest of their journey would be on foot, it would be hard going, they'd be in a foreign country without official sanction, and Wiggo was not helping.

The complaints had started back in Lossiemouth at the briefing.

The colonel had been clear enough.

"You're on your own on this one, John. We can't offer air support; the Libyans are a suspicious lot at the best of times, and if they find out that we're running an op behind their backs they'll go ballistic, maybe literally so."

As soon as Banks got the squad together in the mess and explained the situation, his sergeant began taking it as a personal affront.

"The fucking Sahara?" Wiggo said. "I thought we were going on leave? Fuck, even Largs would do... a few pints, a couple of fish suppers and a wee warm lass at the disco would do me just fine. Anywhere...just no' the fucking Sahara. Have we no' had our fair share of fucking shitty deserts yet? Is that it?"

Even after Banks gave Wiggo 'the look' he could tell that the sergeant wasn't best pleased. On the flight over, Banks gave him the speech about duty, the squad, and the service.

"Bugger me, Cap, I don't need the newbie's speech. I get it. You ken that. I wouldnae be here otherwise," Wiggo said. "The needs of the many outweigh the needs of the few and all that shite. But why is it that we are always the fucking few?"

"I can only give you another quote in return. Ours is not to reason why."

"Do or die? Aye, there's a great choice right there. There had better no' be any fucking monsters this time out, that's all I'm saying."

Banks laughed.

"Nane that I know of. A team of researchers have gone missing and the brass think they've strayed into Libyan territory. We've to get them out and be quiet about it."

"Quiet? That'll make a wee change then. And these researchers? What were they after?"

"An ancient city; a legend. Nobody even knows if it ever existed."

"I knew it. I bloody well knew it. Mair Indiana Jones shite. Wonderful. Just fucking wonderful."

The complaints had stopped, for a while, during a three card brag game with Davies and Wilkins but now that they were approaching their landing at the desert airstrip, Wiggo had turned the volume up again.

"So this lost city, Cap? Does it have a name or is it really lost?"

"The colonel called it Zerzura," Banks replied. "A fabled white city of an architecture uncommon to Africa, said to have been populated by early white Europeans, possibly Greek or Roman but possibly built by a lost race far older than either."

"Aye, that's a lot of very little to be said, that's for sure. Anything else? Anything concrete?"

"Would you believe treasure?" Banks replied, laughing. "Rubies the size of your fist, emeralds like apples? At least that's according to a mannie who walked out of the desert in the Eighteen-Fifties claiming to have spent some time there. He said the people were friendly, if a bit strange and reclusive, with weird religious habits. What kind of weird was never specified. The colonel did say that there's been several expeditions looking for it over the years since but naebody ever found anything."

"So why this new expedition? Has there been new info come to light?"

"Not that I know of, but it's the same old story we all ken too well; the brass only tells us as much as they think we need to know to get a job done. And what we know is that a team of ten from Edinburgh Uni went missing off the grid a week ago, probably in Libyan territory. We sneak in, we find them, we bring them home. End of story."

"And do we know where to start?"

"I have their last known position. It's going to be a bit of a hike to get there."

"How far is a bit?"

"More than a day, less than a week."

"And nae chance of a camel, I suppose?"

"Ye'd have better luck getting off with that lass fae Largs you mentioned."

They landed five minutes later. The airstrip was little more than a flat piece of packed sand and they had to unload their kit themselves; it wasn't the kind of place to employ baggage handlers. As the plane taxied off to the far end of the makeshift runway, they were deposited beside a small shack manned by a single old Egyptian who looked old enough to have been there since the place was built.

"Two planes in a month," he said in perfect English. "The gods have blessed me."

Over cups of strong dark tea and heady local cigarettes at a shaded table outside the shed, Banks found out that the research team had set off three weeks previously by camel, carrying enough provisions for a month, heading west.

"There is nothing out there but sand and death," the old man said. "I told them that, and I will tell you the same. There is no lost city; it is a tale told by gullible men to even more gullible men in order to part them with their money."

"There are lost people though," Banks said grimly. "They are my only concern."

"Then may Allah guide your steps," the old man said, his last words as he went back to sit in his hut and Banks got the team ready to move out.

They'd done most of the preparation back in Scotland; desert camo gear, canteens, rations and packs as light as possible, eschewing body armor in favor of lighter flak jackets and bringing only a light bedding roll, but each man was still carrying somewhere around sixty pounds above their body weight when ammo and weapons were added in.

"It's going to be tough hiking," Banks said once they were all kitted up. "By my reckoning it's a four or five day walk. It might be less, but then again, it might be more, we can't tell until we see the terrain. We'll travel mainly by night, rest up when it's too hot where we can. And remember, it could be worse, it could be Glencoe in the phishing rain, so think on that before complaining too much."

"Aye, but there's a pub at either end of Glencoe, and the sheep are affectionate," Wiggo said.

"Still pining for that camel are you, Wiggo? Then maybe we should make sure you see it first. Lead us out, due west."

The next complaint came a few hours later, not from Wiggo but from Davies. For the past hour they'd been wading through ankle-deep sand and making slow progress.

"Fucking hell, Cap," the private said. "You were nae kidding about the going. Can you no' get somebody to tarmac this shite over? It would make for easier walking."

"I'll see what I can do," Banks said. He looked ahead to where the land rose onto a rockier plateau. It was in the general direction they needed to be going and it looked like better ground.

"Thataway," he said, pointing.

He was proved right ten minutes later when they clambered up an outcrop and saw firmer footing for the foreseeable distance ahead.

"Tarmac as ordered," he said. 'Don't say I never get you anything."

He checked his watch. Two hours until sunset. Just ahead of them was an overhanging rock shelf forming a natural shelter both from the elements and any prying eyes.

"Okay, lads," he said. "Take a break. We'll camp yonder until after dark then get going under the stars. Smoke them if you've got them."

Wilkins got a brew of coffee going and they broke out the rations; it proved to be a thin chilli-con-carne that tasted of rehydrated tomato soup powder, but it was warm and filling which was all that an old soldier could ask for out in the field. Over a smoke, Wiggo tried to pump him for more information.

"So is this really just Indiana Jones level shite, or do you think there's something solid in this lost city bollocks?"

"You ken as much as I do, Wiggo," he said. "The colonel was even less forthcoming than usual about this one. There's a political game getting played upstairs with the Libyan government but I try not to show any enthusiasm for that side of things in front of the old man; he might take it the wrong way and promote me out of the squad."

"We cannae have that, sir. I've just got you broken in."

Banks laughed, and realised at the same instant that he'd finally started to think of Wiggo as his sergeant, rather than the corporal he'd been until recently. He'd always miss auld Hynd; they'd been together too many years, and had been too much like brothers for him to be easily replaced. But Wiggo was proving to be a more than adequate companion, despite his foul mouth and mostly good-natured moaning.

"Don't worry, Wiggo," he replied. "I intend to be ordering you sad sacks around for a while yet; I'm the only one they could get who would believe the shite this squad has got up to in recent years."

"Amen to that, Cap," Wiggo replied. "Let's just hope it's just a wee quiet walk in an admittedly sandy park this time around. That would make a nice change."

"It would at that, Sarge," Banks answered, and saw Wiggo's little smile of pride at the acknowledgement of his rank.

At least they were starting in a good enough mood.

-DAVIES-

"This is much better," Davies said. They'd rested under the overhanging rock for three hours as the desert went dark in front of them and now they walked under a brilliant carpet of stars with the Milky Way stretched in an arc almost immediately overhead. The ground was harder underfoot; it no longer felt like wading in warm treacle and Davies soon got into the old familiar loping gait that came from arduous training carrying heavy packs in the Scottish and Welsh Highlands.

"I bet the Cap is happy to meet your approval," Wilkins said sarcastically.

Wiggo and the captain were some ten yards ahead, so Davies kept his voice low so that only he and Wilkins could hear.

"What about that shite the cap came out with earlier? Do you think he'd take promotion out of the squad? I don't know if I'd want to dae this without him in charge."

"Who knows," Wilkins replied. "Wiggo thinks one of us is definitely some kind of monster magnet though. Maybe it's the cap? He's been at it the longest."

"Awa' and don't talk shite, man. It's just bad luck we keep getting into the weird stuff."

"Bad luck, or destiny? Is there a difference?"

"Oh, so it's destiny is it now? Well you're destined to get a boot up the arse if you don't stop it with this auld bollocks."

"Promises, promises," Wilkins said.

They might joke about it, but Davies knew that Wilkins was as baffled as any of them as to why they kept encountering what Wiggo called 'all this X-Files shite' on every mission. Every time they left base they hoped this would be the time their luck changed and they'd get something straightforward to contend with. Hell, Davies would be happy if it was a squad of Libyan commandos; at least he'd know how to deal with them. Constantly having to appraise the threats posed by monsters of unknown origin had a nasty habit of stretching nerves to breaking point and beyond.

"I didn't sign up for this shite," Davies said under his breath. Wilkins heard him, and laughed.

"Join the army, meet interesting monsters, and shoot the fuck out of them. Would make a great recruitment poster for the videogame generation though, wouldn't it?"

"I cannae see it getting too many Easterhouse lads out of their bedrooms these days."

Davies had been raised in a block of flats in Glasgow's East End, son of a second-generation Jamaican immigrant mother and a father who'd buggered off before Davies knew him. It was a harsh baptism for a wee black lad with a big mouth, but his mother had always been there, always pushed him. She wanted him to be a doctor, he wanted to be a soldier...and now he got to do both,

9

with a group of men as tight as brothers who he trusted with his life. For all his own moaning about monsters he wouldn't choose to be anywhere else.

They walked for several hours under the stars. Every so often Davies spotted the captain check his GPS then change their direction slightly. They appeared to be heading towards a canyon several miles distant. An hour later Captain Banks stopped them on a ridge that looked down over its entrance.

"Welcome to Libya, lads," he said. "If you see passport control, feel free to ignore it. We go canny from here on in; we're not supposed to be here, remember?"

They had a smoke while the captain checked out the terrain ahead.

"If anybody is waiting for us, that's a perfect place for an ambush," Davies said.

"Unfortunately for us, it's the best route to get where we want to go. The alternative is to go all the way round these cliffs and that'll add another day's hard slog," Banks replied. "I can't see anything that could bother us, so we go in, fast and quiet."

"That's the Sarge fucked then," Wilkins said, and Davies was glad it wasn't him that got Cap's evil eye in reply.

After that it was all business for another hour as they made their way down into the canyon. Nothing moved in the night but them, the only sound coming from the soft pad of their feet on rock, the only light coming from the stars and the moon rising at their backs. They ran at a steady trot and Davies thought the Cap was right; it was preferable to a winter's day in the Scottish Highlands, even given the chance there might be a sniper somewhere above watching their every move.

But they reached the canyon with no interference. The walls loomed high above on either side and it was much darker here but they eschewed any lights and continued to move in deeper, slowing to a walk and following the captain in the lead. The only light was the occasional faint blue glare when he checked the GPS on his watch. Finally, after two hours more, he brought them to a halt in the shade of another overhang.

"Take five, lads. Have a smoke if you like, but cup the tips; I think we're alone but best to take no chances."

It was while they were standing in a group smoking that they heard it, the distinctive bray of a camel, somewhere in the night ahead of them, and some distance away.

"It proves nothing," the captain said. "The beasts run wild in these parts; doesn't mean anything."

All the same, when they moved out again, they moved more cautiously.

Davies was bringing up the rear when they heard the camel bray again, closer now, and still ahead of them deeper in the canyon. The captain stopped them to check the area ahead through his rifle sight.

"Two hundred yards, straight ahead and coming this way," he said. "I can just about see it.

It looks like it's carrying a load, but it's on its own. I think it's an escapee."

"Escapee from what?" Wiggo said, but didn't get a reply. Instead the captain moved them out again, and two minutes later they came across the source of the braying.

The beast, on seeing the men approach, made straight for them, as if happy for the company. Davies caught it by the halter and ran a hand across its neck. His palm came away sticky, coated black in the starlight, and he smelled a distinctive odor.

"It's injured," he said. "It's bleeding."

Wiggo checked the beast from head to flank.

"The beast's fine," he said. "It's not its blood. It's been splashed by something...or somebody...else."

"Bring it with us," the captain said. "We need to examine it but not here in the open. It'll be dawn soon so we need to find cover."

It fell to Davies to take the halter. The beast came meekly with him, although he was only too aware of the stink rising off it. It carried packs on either side behind the hump and they appeared to be fully laden but Davies knew better than to have a surreptitious check on the contents; the cap reserved that for himself, it had been obvious from his tone.

The sky above the canyon walls had started to lighten when the captain brought the squad to a halt again. He drew them into one of the numerous box canyons on the southern side, up to the far end where they'd be in deep shade most of the day.

"Get your heads down, lads. I'll take first watch," the captain said, and took the halter from Davies. The private really wanted to stay with the beast to see what it was carrying but the captain led it a few yards out into the canyon to allow the rest of the squad to bed down, and again Davies knew better than to open his mouth. He hoped one day to get some of the privileges that came with rank, but until then silence was definitely the best policy. Wiggo had bucked that trend; his cheeky chappie routine coming with enough genuine charm to override its impertinence. Davies knew himself well enough to know that he would never be able to pull that off without looking like a complete idiot.

Better to keep your mouth shut and be thought a bampot than to open it and prove it.

He only realised how tired he was after he unrolled his bedding. He lay down, closed his eyes, and was asleep almost immediately.

-BANKS-

The first thing Banks did was to examine the blood at the camel's neck, a long, crescent-shaped splash, drying now but only a few hours old at a guess. If it was human, it meant that there might be hope that the research team weren't too far distant, but might be injured. He itched to be on the move; every minute might be important. But traveling too far, too fast, in too much heat, was only going to sap their strength, and their will come to that. The squad would be no use to the researchers if they themselves needed rescuing. They'd all, Banks included, be better off resting now in case tough action was needed later.

After giving the camel some water from his canteen, Banks studied the contents of the packs it had been carrying, emptying them out and laying them on the ground like the pieces of a puzzle he might be able to solve.

There was a large goatskin of water, three bedding rolls, changes of underwear for both men and women and a smaller canvas rucksack containing an expensive digital camera and lenses, a laptop, several notebooks and pens and several pages, obviously torn from an old journal that looked out of place among the modernity.

The camera was full of images of the trip up to that point. Scrolling backwards through them was like seeing the journey they'd taken in reverse; scenic views of the same canyon they were now in, gear being packed onto camels at the old Egyptian's shack and finally fresh-faced smiling faces at railway stations and airports. He went forward through the photos again, looking for any clue as to what might have befallen the research team. The last photograph was an open view out of a canyon across desert dunes to a shimmering oasis in the distance. He searched the camera's internal memory in vain, but there were no more clues.

At least I know they got this far, and a wee bit further.

The laptop was no help either; the machine was password protected and Banks didn't have a clue where to start unlocking it. Davies or Wilkins would be able to hack into it but they needed their sleep. It would have to wait.

By this time the camel had settled down onto the ground and appeared to be contentedly asleep. Banks walked out to the end of the box canyon and looked out. Daylight filled the main ravine and heat washed through it in waves that set the whole scene in front of him rippling. He retreated back into the shade, sat beside the camel and lit a smoke before turning to the notebooks.

Again they didn't tell him anything he didn't know; they were written in a neat hand, by one of the female research team and were a diary of the trip. Once again he went forward in time with them, from organization at Edinburgh Uni then via trains and airplanes to a meeting with the old Egyptian at the airstrip; the diarist had been charmed by him, and was especially appreciative of his tea. The last entry mentioned a stop in one of these box canyons and spoke of her excitement for the days ahead and her hopes of marvels to be seen when they reached the lost city, of which she did not seem to have any doubt. It was dated more than a week ago and there were no more recent entries.

In desperation for any clue at all as to the team's fate Banks finally turned to the old journal pages, although he did not hold out hope for much enlightenment. It was pages from a diary of a British Army sergeant over a hundred and thirty years ago and despite himself, Banks was immediately riveted.

-THEN-

The colonel had been most insistent at our briefing. His colour was up, redness at his cheeks and for once it had nothing to do with the claret he'd taken at dinner the night before. We'd lost three men the night before to insurgents that had got into our encampment, slit the sleeping soldiers' throats in their bunks, then vanished without leaving a trace. He was more than angry. He was furious, taking the deaths as a personal affront to his command.

"Get a squad up into them hills and scout about. We need to know where those buggers are hiding. There will be no repeat of last night's bloody slaughter. I want them found and I want them dead. Don't come back until that job is done."

The buggers were probably Bedouin and more used to hiding in the desert than we were at walking in it but the colonel didn't give a toss about that. And for once I actually agreed with him—you didn't murder a Scotsman in his bed and get away with it. Not if there were any other Scotsmen left to avenge them.

So it was late that Saturday that our squad set off—on foot, none of us trusted those bloody camels—for the range of hills in the desert to the south and west of us. The sun was still up as we departed and little of the day's heat had dissipated. It was hard going. Wearing the kilt meant that at least I had some air around my nethers but the red serge tunic on top felt like a tight corset around my ribs, slowly boiling me from the inside out. What with that and the backpacks—and the Lee Enfields for the men—it was a long tough slog through the sand for all twelve of us. Even our C.O., Lieutenant Timkins—a fresh faced young English gentleman not long out of Sandhurst who hadn't been here long enough to get leathery like the rest of us— seemed to be sweating and somewhat discomforted although he was too much of an officer to show it.

My old pal, Mac—Private MacLeod—had the worst of it—not only was he carrying the same as the rest of us, along with about a stone of extra fat in his belly, he was further burdened by having to carry the bagpipes in his pack. He had complained bitterly for more than a mile until I told him to put a bung in it.

"It could be worse, Mac," I said.

"How's that, Sarge?"

I pointed at our other travelling companion— an old knackered donkey that was being forced to carry our ammo, water and tents.

"I could give you his job if you like?"

"If I can have his todger, I can start now," Mac replied and the subsequent laughter did much to lift our mood, although we were soon enough back to trudging through the endless sand.

We finally reached the hills and made our camp that first night as the last of the sun went from the sky. The pipes gave out a squeal as Mac dropped his pack at the side of the fire. The men and I ate some dried biscuits and got some tea brewing—the Lieutenant didn't join us, staying in his tent, where we could see him bent over, writing up his report. The plan was to get a couple of hours sleep then walk up into the hills before the morning sun got too high in the sky but the trouble started almost as soon as we got our heads down after a smoke.

I'd put Jennings on guard—stout lad, never gave me any lip. I'd served with him in the Sudan on two previous campaigns—I'd seen him stand up against arrows, spears, rifle fire and cavalry charges. So I knew there was something far wrong when he screamed—high pitched, like a boy more than a man—full of fear and pain, his terror carrying far over the small camp in the still desert air.

He was still screaming when I got to the spot where he should be—only he wasn't there—the screams were now coming from higher up in the hills, getting farther away by the second until fading completely somewhere high above us. I tried to make out a landmark we might use to begin a search but there was only a dark, looming cliff face and no distinguishing features.

Even then some of the lads were keen on mounting a search party but the lieutenant put the mockers on that idea.

"Blundering around in the dark isn't going to get us anywhere. There'll be a moon in an hour—we'll go then—and we'll all go together."

I was forced to agree with his decision, although that hour, spent as it was breaking camp then smoking round the remnants of the fire, was one of the longest I have ever spent. At every lull in conversation I listened, expecting a cry from a returning Jennings. But all I heard, echoing in my head if nowhere else, was the memory of the screams and the pain I could hear in them.

I'll give Timkins one thing—he was right about the moon coming up. That was about the last thing he got right that night.

Once there was light, of a sort, we examined the ground where Jennings had been keeping watch. We found his Lee Enfield—bayonet still attached, no blood on the blade and a round in the breech. When they had got him, they'd done it fast. There were only scuffle marks on the sand and surrounding rocks—nothing to indicate the identity of any assailant. All we had was the fact that his screams had faded higher up the hill.

"Right, lads," Timkins said, taking the lead. "Let's find our Corporal Jennings."

At that stage, we were only too happy to comply. We followed—of necessity taking single file due to the almost precarious nature of the cliff path—heading upward, always up.

It proved to be hard going, steep and precipitous in places and it had me wondering just how someone—anyone—could have got Jennings—a big man—up this path while subduing him at the same time. I still hadn't seen any tracks, nor had I spotted any indication that anyone apart from us had passed this way. Despite the cold desert night, I was starting to work up a sweat and my calf muscles screamed in agony with every step. From a distance the hills hadn't looked too daunting but now that we were among them I was wishing we were still back on the sand—it might have been soft but at least it was mostly level.

We kept going up, until even the young lieutenant was forced to admit that tiredness was getting the better of him and allowed us a stop on a ledge for a breather and a smoke.

I ended up next to Mac again and he was still complaining.

"What's that stupid bugger Jennings got himself into this time? Remember when he thought he was in love with that dancing girl in Cairo? Or the lass who turned out to be a boy in Valletta? I'm betting it's something like that again, just you wait and see."

I remembered both tales well—and both had ended in raucous laughter, not pained, wild screams. I held my peace—I'd learned early that a sergeant who shared his worries with the men wasn't much of a sergeant at all. I smoked a Capstan and looked down over the desert—the lights of our encampment in the oasis of Farafra glittered on the horizon—it was what passed for hearth and home during our tour and looked ever more enticing by the minute. It was a struggle to turn back and face the hill—but Jennings was still up there somewhere and we don't leave our men behind.

We climbed again and as it turned out we were nearer our goal than we might have thought. The trail opened out—I was just behind the lieutenant so was among the first to see it—the path led across a flat area between high cliffs into a long, dark narrow valley. Unlike the sight of our home over the desert sands, this did not look the least bit enticing at all. The hairs at the back of my neck rose in the long familiar tingle of dread—I'd been a soldier long enough to recognize a possible ambush when I saw one.

"We should take this slowly, sir," I said to the lieutenant, keeping my voice low so the men wouldn't hear. "I don't like the look of it at all."

"Nonsense," the lieutenant said, loud enough for the men—and anybody else in that damned valley—to hear. "We are on the Queen's business and we shall do as we damn well please."

And with no further ado he started to stride away from me along the path and into the valley. I waited for ten seconds to see if anybody would shoot him for me before I followed.

We found the city a minute later.

The moonlight, such as it was, did little to light this end of the valley but it was enough to show us that the buildings that filled the whole west end were of great age—and great magnificence. A crescent outer wall stretched across forty yards of valley floor and was half as high again, with only a single high arched passage as entry. Behind that we saw that a city of high turrets and magnificent balconies marched away upwards the canyon, gaining height until the tallest of them were level with the highest walls at the top of the canyon.

The outer wall was of the same sandstone we were used to seeing on the small local buildings in the towns but these were blocks ten, twelve feet or more square, aligned so seamlessly it was difficult to see where they were joined. The outer surface of the wall was covered, ground to as high as we could see in the gloom, with fine miniature carvings that at first glance seemed to depict scenes of battles of antiquity but would have taken someone with more intellect—and patience—than I to unravel. At that moment I was only interested in getting the squad off the valley floor and under some cover, to a spot where ambush wouldn't be quite so easily accomplished.

Lieutenant Timkins, seemingly without a care in the world, was already making his way in through the archway. I left two men at the entrance gate—Jock Benson and Andy Hynd, stout lads the both of them and able to keep each other alert—and herded the rest of the squad inside.

The arch was more than fifteen feet tall and the wall through which it passed was about the same thickness, a testament to the solidity of the vast structure. We walked along the short corridor and inside the entranceway to the city itself. Dust lay underfoot—our footprints showed clearly—as did something else—strange scuffed marks, similar to those I had seen at the spot where Jennings had been taken—there were a great many of them, covering all the ground I could see in the dim light.

We found the lieutenant trying to light a wall sconce with his tinderbox. MacLeod managed it rather more quickly, using up half a dozen of his safety matches in the process but finally we had the sconce—and several others on opposite walls-lit, providing more than enough light to illuminate the interior of this entrance hall. A wide left-hand corridor opened out into some kind of temple.

That structure was little more than one large hall with a high vaulted rock roof curving far overhead. The whole thing was supported by twin rows of giant columns that stretched back against the cliff, narrowing where the box canyon into which it was built came to a point until, at the far end some thirty yards and more away, stood a tall, monstrous statue. It was carved of a single slab of black stone that seemed to swallow all light. As we stepped closer, I saw it did not, as I had first thought, depict a man wearing some kind of cape but was in fact a giant beetle, its carapace half-opened, its head raised high to where the single gleaming black pincer seemed to scrape the roof. Behind the statue, going up, high up the sheer rock face, there was a set of stone steps carved into the cliff, steeper than any path we had yet traversed and if there was an end to them, I couldn't see it in the dark.

We found Jennings—what was left of him—lying at the foot of the statue. His body looked strangely sunken and when I got closer I saw, all too clearly—the reason—the poor chap had been eviscerated—his kilt was in tatters and his serge tunic ripped open—but not as torn as his belly. His flesh had been brutally sundered. His insides—guts, liver, stomach, heart and all were gone, as if scooped out. Then another thought struck me—one that made me glad that I had only partaken of tea and biscuits, although I almost lost both anyway. He looked like he had been eaten—and that he'd been alive for at least some of the time it was happening.

I heard the lieutenant sob at my back and Mac had taken to cursing, none too quietly, his brogue echoing and whispering around us, coming back from above like a chorus of praying monks. I called them both to quiet—I had heard something else, something I couldn't quite recognize, a high keening drone, almost as if Mac was starting up on the pipes. It was coming from some distance—but it was definitely getting closer.

I peered up to the steps behind the statue—it seemed that I felt fresher air in my face as I did so—but the sound wasn't coming from there—it was coming from outside, out in the valley. And it was most definitely getting louder.

-BANKS-

That was the full extent of the pages from the journal; it had him hooked right enough, and he was eager to know the rest of the tale, but he could only hope to learn the Victorian squad's fate at some later date. Besides, he shouldn't even have been reading it in the first place. Not paying attention while on watch was something he'd have chewed any of the others out about; now wasn't the time for sloppy soldiering.

He put the journal pages with the notebooks and camera and refilled the packs save for the laptop that he left for the privates to unlock. Then he took his smokes and went to stand at the mouth of the box canyon, where he should have been all along.

Even then his mind wouldn't let it be, his thoughts returning back to that other Scottish squad out looking for trouble, and finding it. He wondered about one of the names, Andy Hynd. Sure, it wasn't an uncommon surname in the West of Scotland, but the juxtaposition between the one in service back then and his recently retired friend now was too much to ignore and it was something he'd be chasing up when they got home. If nothing else it would be a tale to tell his old pal over a beer or three.

He forced his concentration to more pressing matters but even those harked back to the journal; he intended to head for the very same oasis that had been the Victorian squad's regimental headquarters.

Would they find evidence of that long ago encampment? Or, as he hoped, would he find evidence, or even the team themselves, of the more recent research expedition?

The camel was a puzzle though. It had obviously escaped from that expedition. But where had the blood come from? And why had nobody tracked it down and retrieved it, given how docile it was around people?

The questions were still whirling in his head when Wiggo came to relieve him several hours later.

"There's coffee in the pot, Cap," he said. "Davies is up next after me."

Before leaving, Banks had a smoke with the sergeant and told him about the journal, and the names he'd read there."

"Hynd? A coincidence, do you think?"

"Maybe aye, maybe no," Banks replied. "We both ken that the service runs in Frank's family a long way back. Maybe he had a great-great grandad who served in these parts. If we get lucky, we might find out more for ourselves further down the line here. In the meantime, look after this camel here; it might have more stories to tell us."

"I'll try not to scare her off," Wiggins said with a smile.

"That'll be another first, then," Banks replied, and headed for his bedroll.

When he woke the sky was darkening from the east. It was still blisteringly hot in the box-canyon but they'd all rested, they hadn't been attacked...and the camel hadn't run off. Banks counted that as a small victory. He joined the others in a quick breakfast.

Wilkins and Davies had between them hacked into the laptop but hadn't found anything of note more than they knew already. The same photos he'd seen on the camera had been loaded up onto the hard drive and there were several emails home but they all stopped at the oasis that was their next destination.

"I guess we'll have to do it the hard way," Banks said then had the squad make ready to move out.

When they headed west out of the box canyon into the main ravine the camel showed its first signs of recalcitrance; it obviously disproved of going back the way it had come and pulled hard against Davies' hand on the halter.

"Something's got her spooked, Cap," the private said, but Banks could see that clearly enough for himself.

What are we getting ourselves into this time?

Over the next couple of hours Banks heard Davies mutter curses at the camel, imprecations to get it moving. At least it was still with them, for now, but it had begun to bray in annoyance, threatening to give away their position to anyone who might be looking out for them. Finally Banks had heard enough. He went back to the beast, retrieved the camera and notebook which he put in his own pack, then gave it a whack on the rump.

"Away you go then," he said. "We'll no' keep a lassie where she's no' comfortable."

"Speak for yourself," Wiggo said.

The camel brayed, almost a laugh, in reply then was off and away, heading east in long loping strides. She was soon lost in the gloom. The canyon echoed briefly with the sound of her movement then fell quiet.

They had a smoke and water break at midnight.

"By my reckoning we're halfway to where this opens out to desert again," Banks said. "Then it's a couple of hours slog across sand to the oasis."

"And after that?" Wiggo asked.

"Two days west into the hills. Maybe three."

"And the same slog on the way back, maybe with sick or wounded?" Davies added.

"Aye," Banks said. "If you were thinking this is a cushy number, think again. If we push on, we could be at yon oasis by daybreak. I promise you a longer rest there."

Banks' estimate proved about right. Four hours more in the ravine brought them to the point where it opened out again onto a sea of dunes. There was a darker shadow on the western horizon which he guessed must be the oasis, but that wouldn't be certain until daylight, and he hoped to be there by then.

"Come on, lads," he said. "Last one at the bar gets the round in."

-DAVIES-

By the time they reached the oasis Davies' calves felt hard as rock and burned as if stabbed with a hot poker. His pack dragged with every step, threatening to tug him back and down onto his arse. Despite the fact that it was not yet full dawn the heat came in intense waves across the dunes. Every breath felt like hot ash in his mouth and nostrils and his head pounded with a hangover-sized ache.

All of that was forgotten when they crested the last dune and looked down on the oasis.

Davies' knowledge of deserts came mainly from old Hollywood movies. As such he had expected a small concave hollow ringed by palm trees with a wee blue pool of water, perfectly circular of course, in the center. Instead he looked down over a verdant valley the size of a major town. Yes, there were pools, yes they were blue, but there were scores of them dotted amid swaying palms and ferns in an undulating landscape pockmarked with rocky outcrops. A camel trail led down from where they stood and when Davies' gaze followed it led directly to a small clump of tents around one of the aforesaid pools several hundred yards west of where the squad stood. Lifting his head and looking up gave a view west past the oasis. A mountain chain shimmered in the dawn, twenty miles and more distant.

Banks stopped the squad at the top of the dune and had them lie prone while he used his rifle sight to check out the camp.

"No sign of movement," he said. "But maybe they're sleeping. You ken how much these Uni types like their kip. No sudden noises, lads. We don't want them spooked like yon camel. If we wake somebody up unexpectedly they might shoot first and ask questions later."

The squad went down the dune in single file, taking care not to disturb the sand into an avalanche. They needn't have bothered; it was obvious long before they reached the camp that there had been trouble.

Several of the tents were no more than tattered shreds. Clothing and equipment was strewn across a wide area, as if picked up then tossed aside. One of the tents, the largest of the group, contained two overturned trestles. A firepit in the center was long cold, the blood spatter on the inside walls and ceiling dried to a brown crust.

They didn't find a single body.

"Inventory," Banks said to Wiggo. "I want a record of everything here. Shout if you find anything that'll shed light on what happened."

Davies went with Wiggo to the west end of the encampment while the captain and Wilkins searched around the main tent. They still didn't find any bodies but they found plenty of disturbed sand in a trail heading west, pointing directly towards the mountain range they'd seen from the dunes.

Davies bent to examine the area.

"What do you make of this, Sarge?"

Scratched tracks, grooved and pitted, led away from the tents and off west, many of them, but neither Davies or Wiggo could conceive how they were made. There were no footprints, no camel tracks, just a tangled web of grooves and scratches.

Davies looked up to the hills.

"Whatever it was, it went thataway," he said.

"Aye. And took something with it. I've got more blood here too."

"What the fuck happened here, Sarge?"

"Buggered if I know, lad. Let's hope the others have had better luck."

Davies followed Wiggo back to the heart of the encampment and found the captain and Wilkins poring over a small cork board with a map pinned to it. Beside the map was a list of ten names, split into two clusters, six and four. An arrow pointed from the group of six off to a spot high in the mountain range to the west.

"Looks like this group went ahead to suss out the area while four stayed here to make a base camp," the captain said.

"But where are they?" Wilkins asked.

The captain looked grim.

"Look around you, lad. There's been enough blood spilled here to account for them. As for who, or what, did it, I'm open to suggestions. It wasn't a gunfight, there's no sign of a struggle. Whatever happened, it went down fast."

"And they were taken off west, if we're reading the track right," Wiggo added.

They went back to the spot where the tracks left the camp. The sun was up now and the heat was rising fast. The captain looked at the tracks and sucked his teeth. He looked up at the mountains, then at the sun.

"You're right, Sarge," he said. "They went this way. We don't know whether they were taken alive or not but at least one of them was bleeding, so we'll hope for the best. I was planning on a rest here for the daylight hours, but I'm going to ask that we press on; if anybody survived, they could be in sore need of our help."

Davies joined the others in mock groaning but like the captain they all knew it was the only choice. They'd come here on a rescue mission; sitting on their arses wasn't an option.

It was going to be a hard slog; the trail rose upward out of the camp and within minutes they were on a rocky path that wended its way through the other reaches of the oasis and rose sharply into stony foothills with no places to provide respite from the sun. The only consolation was that the ground was firm underfoot and Davies was able to at least regain the practised loping stride that kept the pack from dragging at his shoulders.

They climbed in silence for twenty minutes before the captain called for a rest break. He'd stopped on a flatter ledge. There were more of the scratches and gouges here, and more spatter of dried blood.

"At least we're on the right track," he said.

"Any idea where they might be going, Cap?" Davies asked.

The captain explained about the old journal entry.

"The description in there matches what we've done so far and where we might be going." He pointed off west. The mountains were closer now, shimmering in the heat.

Davies thought he could just make out a darker patch that might be a ravine or valley but it was still too far to be sure. Whatever it was, it seemed like a long walk was yet ahead of them.

They rested for twenty minutes, trying to find shade behind some of the larger rocks. Davies sipped at his water; it was getting warm and felt thicker on his tongue.

"I could murder a cold pint," he said, and Wiggo laughed.

"Well, you were last into the oasis, so the first round's on you," he said. "I'll have two."

"And a packet of cheese and onion," Wilkins added.

As usual even a bout of light banter did a lot for their spirits but they were soon dampened again.

The captain called them to their feet. As Davies stood, he thought he heard a high whistle in the wind. He was about to remark on it when he saw the others had heard it too, and the sound quickly grew in both depth and volume into a loud screeching drone that echoed around the foothills only to die off as quickly as it had come.

"What the fuck was that?"

Wiggo did not look happy.

"Fucked if I know. But I'll lay you two to one that it's the same bloody thing that took the people we're after. And I'll also give you even money it's a fucking monster."

-BANKS-

Banks had to stop them before noon. The climb had been strenuous, the baking heat unrelenting, and if there was to be a firefight at the end of it, they needed to be in good enough shape for it. He found one of the few shaded spots in the lee of an outcrop and allowed the squad to flop down in it.

"We'll stay here until dusk," he said. "Get some rest, sleep if you can. You deserve it; that was a long haul."

"Shall we set watch?" Wiggo asked.

"Same as before," he replied. "I'll take first dibs as I was last up out of my kip this morning. Get some water in you, get your heads down. If we crack on hard overnight my reckoning is we'll be there...wherever there is...by morning."

Before bedding down they all ate a meal from their rations and washed it down with some freshly brewed coffee; he limited them all to one cup each, not knowing how long they'd have to eke out their water. Davies and Wilkins were asleep almost immediately, but Wiggo came to join Banks for a smoke in a shaded spot looking back downhill over the shimmering oasis on the horizon.

"Do you think we'll find anybody?" the sergeant asked.

"We'll find them. Whether we find them alive...that's a different story. There was a fuckload of blood back in yon camp."

"Aye. That's what's got me thinking. Too much blood; somebody, maybe all of them, died down there. So why take the bodies?"

"Don't dwell on it, Sarge. We'll find out when we find out."

"Now you're starting to sound like auld Hynd," Wiggo said.

"So I should. I taught him everything he knew."

Their soft laughter echoed around them.

It was answered by another whistling drone from higher up in the hills.

Banks' watch passed uneventfully. There was no recurrence of the droning noise and nothing moved in the view over the oasis save the shimmering heat haze above the foliage. His thoughts turned again and again to the fate of the researchers but, as he had told Wiggo, they'd find out when they found out, and no amount of speculation was going to get him anywhere. Instead he allowed himself to fall into that half-dreaming, half-watching state that had served him well for many years on guard duties all over the world, trusting his instincts and reflexes to warn him if action was needed.

He felt almost rested when Wiggo arrived mid-afternoon to take a spell, but fell immediately into sleep on laying down on his bedroll.

He came out of it in darker shadow, woken by a recurrence of the droning noise. It was louder now, somehow more insistent, and seemed to come not from one particular spot but from both above and below them on the hillside.

Davies was on guard, weapon raised when Banks joined him to look down the valley.

"Trouble, lad?"

"Buggered if I know, sir," Davies replied. "There was only one sound at first, then another joined it. The one down the hill is definitely getting louder."

The noise had an unworldly, ethereal quality to it, slightly rasping and almost metallic, more like something produced by a synthesised sound effect rather than anything natural.

Wiggo and Wilkins arrived to join them. The sound continued to increase in volume, the noise from below them joined now by an increasing chorus of overlapping drones from higher up.

"Fuck me, it's a pipe band warming up," Wiggo said. That had Banks thinking again about the Victorian era squad, and bagpipes and abducted men.

"Form up," he said. "And eyes open. I don't think it's friendly."

They all had their weapons in hand and moved to stand in the open, back to back with each man taking a quadrant. Banks had the view downhill and it seemed to him that the droning sound from below had shifted off to his right among a tangled field of tumbled rock. The noise from above got louder, more frantic.

If an attack is coming, it'll be soon.

He saw Wiggo react, almost shoot and decide not to when several small rocks shifted over on the right and a trickle of sand fell between them. Then, as quickly as it had come, the sound faded and died, leaving them alone on a quiet hillside.

"Whatever it was, it got past us," Davies said.

"Aye," Banks replied. "And they had us outflanked and outnumbered. Why didn't they attack?"

"Maybe we just got checked out?" Wiggo said.

"Aye, maybe. And if that's the case, they got an advantage; they saw us and we didn't see them. We still don't know what we're up against here. What do you say, lads? Shall we crack on and see if we can see the rabbit?"

"Lead on," Wiggo said. "But if Tim the Enchanter shows up, I'm for the off."

Davies and Wilkins both laughed, but the allusion, like many of Wiggo's pop culture references, passed Banks by. He let it wash over him unremarked; he'd found that was usually for the best where his sergeant's attempts at wit were concerned.

"Five minutes then," he said. "Get your gear. We've got more climbing to do."

Dusk was settling on the hillside as they moved out again. They kept tighter order now, alert for any shifting shadows as they reached the edge of the foothills and entered the mountains proper. After an hour's climb he brought the squad to a halt again. They were on a ledge overlooking the oasis away on the horizon which was now merely a darker patch of shadow. Near the edge of the ledge was remnants of an old campfire, the circle of stones long gone cold.

Long indeed, he thought. *This must be where they lost the corporal, Jennings.*

"Smoke them if you've got them, lads," he said. "But keep your wits about you. Nobody more than six feet from anybody else at all times and if you need a pish, do it here. No wandering off."

He looked up the hill at the trail ahead. It looked to be steeper up there, more precipitous, and he remembered the old journal mentioning areas of single file climbing. He searched in vain for an alternative route, some other way around, but it seemed the only way was directly up.

"Okay, lads," when he finished his smoke, "one last big push and we'll be at the rescue site by morning. With any luck we'll be able to cadge breakfast off the researchers and start making our way straight back home."

"Luck?" Wiggo said. "I've forgotten the meaning of the word."

"To be fair, Sarge," Wilkins said, "there's plenty of words you never knew the meaning of in the first place."

"I've got two for you, lad," Wiggo replied. "Bugger, and off."

When they headed out a minute later, Banks once again took the lead.

It got steeper almost immediately and they were soon into the single file climbing that was mentioned in the old journal pages. It never got to the stage where he needed to resort to using his hands for balance but it was a close thing in places, and he was all too aware that a momentary lapse in concentration would overbalance him and help the weight of his pack carry him backwards into a long, possibly fatal, fall down the cliff face. His whole attention was on the trail ahead and he never raised his gaze from more than six feet ahead at any one time, trusting his feet to follow.

They climbed in silence in that manner for what seemed like hours while darkness fell around them, filling in the shadows to a greater blackness. Thin clouds scudded overhead, obscuring the stars and darkening the night even further, so much so that Banks was forced to switch on his gun light. He took care to keep it aimed where his gaze had been directed; no more than six feet ahead at any point. But now that it was illuminated, he felt much more exposed and had to remind himself not to speed up to compensate.

He was so intent on concentrating that it took him several seconds to notice something new in the night, not a sound this time, but a smell, an acrid, acid odor akin to the tang of malt vinegar. It persisted for several minutes before it dispersed in the night air, but it had been so singular that Banks made a mental note not to forget it.

You never know what might prove important later.

The single file climb seemed to go on forever but eventually, near midnight, they came to a high wide ledge that allowed them to stop and rest.

Wiggo joined him for a smoke at the cliff edge. They looked down. Banks knew the trail they had taken was down there somewhere, and the oasis beyond that, but the cloud cover ensured that the view was obscured and there was only dark shadow below.

"Give the lads twenty minutes, Cap?" Wiggo asked.

"Make it thirty," he replied. "I need the rest more than they do. This would have been a damned sight easier if I was ten years younger."

"I hear you," Wiggo said. "Ten years, a load of beer and a wheen of smokes certainly makes a difference."

Banks laughed.

"Ah well, at least we've got experience and wisdom on our side."

Wiggo laughed in return.

"Speak for yourself. All I've got going for me is good looks and charm."

"I wouldn't give up the day job, Sarge."

"Do you think I do this for the fun of it?"

"Aye. I think we both do," Banks said and for once Wiggo didn't have a witty comeback; it had been too close to the truth.

-DAVIES-

Davies brought up the rear as they left the high ledge to continue upward. If his guestimate was right, they were now nearing the base of the darker area he'd seen from far below that he'd taken for the entrance to a valley. They must now be a couple of thousand feet higher than the oasis, and it felt like it; the night air was actually cool against his cheeks, and although they were working hard on the climb, he hardly broke sweat.

There had been no further recurrence of the droning wails, for which Davies was thankful, for it had put the willies up him badly enough in daylight.

If I heard it again up here in the dark I might shit myself.

Davies had a love-hate relationship with dark nights. They had been few and far between in his youth, when neon lit the tower blocks and street lighting ruled the city. He actively had to seek out pockets of shadow to hide himself away from his tormentors, of which there had been several. Once he got older, he grew to appreciate the solitude and peace to be found under a blanket of stars but out here in a desert night he felt more like the scared kid from Easterhouse than any searcher of serenity, and he hated it for reminding him.

Back then he'd have been tucked away in a dark corner, listening for pursuit. His ears still served him as well as they did then and although most wouldn't have taken note of it, Davies knew that a tumble of sand and gravel behind him meant trouble. He turned and aimed his weapon down the slope, controlling a desperate urge to let off a few rounds. More sand and gravel moved, accompanied by a soft scraping, almost like metal on rock, no more than ten yards away.

He peered into the shadows, trying to discern any moving patches of deeper darkness, looking for a man-shaped target, but all he saw were the squat, rounded forms of the scattered rocks. The next time the scraping sound came he had to swivel to his left to be facing it, but there was still no discernible target, although there was now a definite tang of vinegar in the air.

He let out two soft whistles to signal Wiggo, the next man above him, that there was trouble. The sergeant was at his back only seconds later.

"There's something here, Sarge," he whispered. "I think we're being followed."

"Let's light him up, give him something to think about," Wiggo said. "Lights on in three… one, two…"

The pair of them switched on their gun lights, both aiming at almost the same spot. All they lit up was what looked like a smooth black domed boulder more than six feet in length and three in height. Before they could take a shot, the boulder grew short stocky legs and scurried away, moving at speed into the deeper shadows leaving behind a spatter of loose sand and the scraping, almost metallic sound.

"Rocks that can run away? Will wonders never fucking cease?" Wiggo said. "You go on ahead of me, lad, I'll watch your back."

As Davies turned back to the hill the high droning sound returned, coming from the direction in which the 'rock' had scurried. It was answered by a chorus of drones from above, then once again the night fell silent.

Even with Wiggo behind and below him Davies felt the darkness at his back, pressing on his shoulders, an almost physical weight. Some neon and street lighting would suit him just fine about now.

They climbed with no further incident for several more hours. The thin cloud dispersed and the sky filled with twinkling light, enough to show them the trail and to cast deeper shadows in the clefts and fissures around them. Davies looked up; they were almost at the mouth of a huge ravine that towered high above, about twenty minutes more climbing at a guess. He looked forward to some respite. All of them were breathing heavily, and their pace had slowed considerably from earlier. Davies knew he had a couple of hours left in the tank but after that he'd be fit for nothing until they had some down time to recuperate. He could only hope that whatever was tracking them would allow them that luxury.

Twenty minutes later his guess was proved right when the captain brought them to a halt where the track widened and a vast ravine opened up before them. Higher up was still cast deep in shadow, but Davies got the impression of regular shapes, straight lines and high towers.

"We're nearly there," the captain said. "I believe that's our 'white city' ahead... a bit further than it looks, maybe half an hour more. There're no lights I can see, no sign of a camp, but if it is indeed a city, they might be inside a building somewhere. We all know we're not alone on this hill, but whatever's on our tail, they're as wary of us as we are of them."

"I wouldnae bet my shirt on that, Cap," Wiggo said.

"Nor me," the captain admitted. "But we've got this far without a firefight. Let's hope we can keep it that way."

He allowed them a smoke break. Davies joined Wilkins to stand on the ledge and look back out over the desert. Far off to the east the sky had started to lighten to signal dawn's approach. That was still an hour or more away, but it looked like the captain had got his sums right; they would be entering the lost city with the coming of dawn at their back.

Half an hour later the first true rays of dawn struck the crescent outer wall of a huge city. The wall stretched across forty yards of the valley floor and was half as high as that again, with only a single high arched passage, a near twenty-foot high semi-circle, as entry. Behind that sat a city of high turrets and crenulated balconies that marched away up the canyon, the turrets gaining height until the tallest of them were level with the highest walls at the top of the canyon which Davies estimated to be another thousand feet or so above. It reminded Davies of some of the fantasy cities in modern movies, and although he knew, historically, it shouldn't be here, it nonetheless also looked perfectly natural in its setting, as if it had always belonged there.

It was built of blocks ten, twelve feet or more square, aligned so seamlessly it was difficult to see where they were joined. The outer surface of the crescent wall was covered, ground to as high as they could see, with fine miniature carvings that at first glance seemed to depict scenes of battles of antiquity although whether they might be Roman, Greek or even older was beyond Davies' education to determine. The whole thing gave an impression of solidity, of ages past that had been endured and survived. It also, to Davies at least, gave off a feeling of emptiness like an immense, perfectly preserved mausoleum. His gut told him that there was nobody alive here for them to find.

The captain led them across the open valley in front of the great wall, a flat, featureless plain that looked to have been purposefully flattened and levelled in some distant past. Davies saw more of the scratches and grooves here, a great many of them. He looked for a blood trail or any evidence that the people from the encampment from the oasis had been brought this way, but there was only bare rock and sand.

They stopped just inside the wide entranceway. Daylight hadn't yet reached the city beyond which still lay in darkness and shadow. The entranceway was an arch set into the wall and was more than twelve feet thick.

"We're all knackered," the captain said. "So let's rest up here for an hour before heading into the city. If anybody was waiting for rescue, they'd be watching and they'd have seen us coming; I think we're alone here. But we need rest before we start exploring. Wiggo, you watch the valley side, I'll watch the city side, Wilkins and Davies, get a brew on, I'm parched."

Making a pot of coffee did a lot to ground Davies back in reality, something he realized he was sorely in need of after the climb in the dark to this lost city of an ancient race.

It's just like Wiggo said. Indiana Jones shite. All we're missing is a bunch of Nazis.

He was getting the stove set up when he noticed several copper-colored things in the sand at his feet. He bent, brushed some dirt aside, and then realized what it was he was looking at. And once he'd spotted one of them, he looked around and saw that the whole area was covered in them.

"Sarge?" he said, calling Wiggo over. "Are these what I think they are?" He took a handful in his palm to show them. "They're spent British .303 rifle cartridges, aren't they? From the old Lee Enfields? Boer War vintage or thereabouts?"

"Aye," Wiggo said after a long look. "It looks like the Cap's Victorian squad story is true enough. They were here, and got into a firefight too by the looks of things. But what the hell were they shooting at?"

"I'm guessing we'll find out soon enough," the captain said from Davies' other side. "Let's not go looking for more trouble than we can afford. How's that coffee coming along?"

After coffee and a smoke Davies felt almost rested and ready. The captain seemed to agree.

"Okay, lads. Let's find our lost lambs if we can. Stay close and stay alert, we don't yet know what we might be up against here."

-BANKS-

Banks led the squad along the short corridor and inside the entranceway to the city itself. More scratches and gouges covered all the ground he could see in the dim light.

Ancient sconces hung on the walls, but they wouldn't need them; the sun was at their backs now, and providing more than enough illumination to show the entrance to a wide left-hand corridor; Banks remembered the Victorian tale and led them through. As he expected, it opened out into some kind of temple, a large hall with a high vaulted rock roof curving far overhead supported by twin rows of giant columns that stretched back against the cliff, narrowing where the box canyon into which it was built came to a point.

At the far end some thirty yards and more away, stood a tall, monstrous statue of a giant beetle. It was carved of a single slab of black stone that seemed to swallow all light but it was what was laid out beneath it that got Banks' attention.

They had found their lost lambs, and more besides by the look of it.

A score of bodies, or what was left of them, lay at the statue's base, laid out in what appeared to be ritualistic fashion, their rib cages burst open and spread, their insides hollowed out and organs removed. Where clothing could be determined, those nearest the door were in modern dress, those nearest the statue wore faded red serge tunics and the remnants of kilts. Banks counted the more recent ones; there were ten, no more, no less.

There was nobody alive here to be rescued.

Banks forced himself to undertake the gruesome task of an inspection of the bodies. The ones clad in the red serge were obviously the mortal remains of the Victorian squad. The more recent could only be the people he'd been sent to look for. From the state of the corpses, they'd all been dead for some time; any blood spilled was long since congealed and dry and the bodies were starting to take on the desiccated look of corpses left out in the sert air.

"What the fuck happened here, Cap?" Wiggo said at his side.

Banks didn't answer at first. He stood away from the dead and looked around the chamber. Off to his left, at the foot of a long flight of stone steps, lay a tumbled mound of discarded clothing, rucksacks, satchels, cameras and laptops, all mingled with rusted Lee-Enfield rifles, British Army issue sabers, empty ammunition boxes and a forlorn set of broken bagpipes.

"Put one of the lads on guard at the door. The rest of us will sift through the pile. Maybe there's something in that lot that'll tell us."

A search through the pile did not yield much that they did not already know; the research team had obviously split into two groups, six had come here, four stayed at the oasis but, by some means as yet unknown, all ten had ended up eviscerated and laid out in front of the black stone idol. Banks set

Wiggins to work on the laptops and cameras in the hope of more info then Wiggo and he turned their attention to the remnants of the Victorian squad's expedition. There was not a lot left to show of them; old bones, used cartridges and rusted weapons. Somehow the bagpipes were the worst, broken and discarded, the airbag rotted in the desert air, a symbol of everything that had gone wrong for them.

"And yet," Banks said softly, "somebody got away."

"How do you make that out, Cap?" Wiggo said.

"Yon old journal entries we found. Somebody wrote them, and they weren't found here, were they? The camel came from the oasis group, not the group that came up into the hills; you'd never get yon beast up that track we climbed in the night."

"So how come the story's news to us? Surely, kenning auld sodgers, somebody would have passed it on over a drink? It would have made it into legend."

"Not unless the man who wrote it never intended for it to be read," Banks said.

Their search through the detritus of old lives was interrupted by a shout from Wilkins.

"I might have something here, Sarge."

They walked over to where the private was crouched over one of the laptops. The casing was battered and cracked but the screen had remained intact and Wilkins had got it working. He showed them a series of photographs; the most recent showed a grinning team of six standing in front of the main entrance gate to the city.

"There's a couple of emails back and forward to the oasis camp too," Wilkins said. "The latest is nearly a week ago. After that, nowt from either end."

"No Mayday calls from either?"

"Nope. Zilch."

"Anything else?"

"Only this," Wilkins said. "It looks like a scanned version of that journal you were telling us about. And you'll want to read the rest of it. I had a quick fly through it. It's relevant."

Wilkins showed Banks how the document reader's page up and down function worked and left him and Wiggo to read while he joined Davies in the doorway.

Banks found the point where the earlier pages had stopped and went on from there. Soon, both he and Wiggo were lost, captured in the old soldier's tale.

-THEN-

I peered up to the steps behind the statue, it seemed that I felt fresher air in my face as I did so, but the sound wasn't coming from there, it was coming from outside, out in the valley. And it was most definitely getting louder.

Benson and Hynd had started shooting before I reached the archway. I saw what they were firing at as I reached their position.

Their target was as black as that statue inside, not quite as large, being only eight feet from tail to pincers, but it was the biggest bloody beetle I ever hoped to see. And it seemed to be very much alive. Moonlight glinted off one pincer that looked as sharp as any razor as it came forward across the valley floor, heading straight for the temple entrance.

"Well don't just stand there, lads," I said to Benson and Hynd. "Shoot the bloody thing again."

Hynd fired, his shot ricocheted off the carapace and left no sign of a wound, and the oncoming beetle did not slow.

"What do you think we've been trying to do, Sarge?" Benson replied, firing another shot that did nothing to stop the approaching beast. By this time the rest of the squad had arrived in the archway entrance. I didn't even have to give the order, they lined up and sent shot after shot at the beetle which finally faltered under the onslaught after two of its front legs were blown out from under it. It collapsed in the dirt, still not dead until I ordered one last volley put into it for good measure. Finally it stopped twitching. In the dark it looked like no more than just another large rock on the ground.

The valley echoed with the shots then fell still and quiet, but not for long. The whine I'd heard earlier, the one that had alerted me to trouble in the first place, started up again, a drone that came from everywhere and nowhere at once, filling the night air with a hum that seemed to set my very bones vibrating inside me.

"What the hell is this shite, Sarge?" Mac said beside me.

"I don't know, lad," I replied. "But get back inside the passage, no sense in making ourselves any bigger targets than we need to."

The squad complied, and just in time as the rocks on the verges of the valley floor started to rise up and creep forward, not rocks at all, but more of the huge black beetles, a great many more, scores of them, all coming our way.

We used the tables from inside the temple as makeshift barricades, getting them up just in time as the valley floor filled up with crawling beetles, varying in size from little more than a foot across to monsters more than ten feet in length and as tall as a man at the height of their domed shells. At first they scarcely seemed interested in us at all. They fed on the one we'd just killed, stripping it to pieces in seconds. When I saw how expertly a large beetle sliced the dead one open with its pincers, I knew exactly what had happened to poor Jennings, and I remembered.

We had found his body inside the temple.

There might be more of these things at our back.

I sent Hynd and Benson to keep an eye on the inside and give them a chance of a break and a smoke while the rest of us lined up against the makeshift barricade. Several of the men needed fresh ammo; I sent Mac to fetch a box from the donkey.

That was all it took. Mac went over toward the beast, the donkey brayed in response, the sound carrying clear across the valley floor, and every one of the beetles outside suddenly took note of our presence. The humming drone rose to a higher pitched whine and now that we were close enough I saw that it was caused by the beasts rubbing their back legs together so fast that they seemed little more than a blur. The sound was eerily spectral, the only thing I had heard that was remotely similar was a wolf pack in the Afghan hills, but this was worse, it felt unnatural, against any law of nature with which I was familiar, setting my teeth on edge and bone of my skull to buzzing.

I had little time to dwell on it however. I was still checking my revolver to ensure I was fully loaded when the beasts attacked our defenses. Fortunately, the squad remembered their drills and waited for my order. I let the beasts approach to some thirty yards distance, then gave the command.

"Aim for the legs. Open fire."

The first volley didn't stop them all, but enough went down to cause a feeding frenzy among the rest as they quickly forgot about us at the sudden availability of something else to eat. A second volley added more carnage to their feast. But I saw little sense in continually feeding what was, after all, our enemy. I ordered the squad to stop firing, the two volleys had already filled the air with the tang of powder and smoke, and my ears rang for long seconds afterward but when things cleared, I still heard the drone, the high whine of the beetles. And although we had indeed felled a dozen or more of their kind, the valley floor still swarmed with them.

But for the moment at least, they seemed to have lost all interest in us again, being fully intent on dismembering and devouring their kith and kin.

"What the bloody hell are those things, Sarge?" Mac asked. He'd already put down his rifle and was lighting up a smoke. I hadn't ordered a stand down, then again, neither had the lieutenant, and it was his job more than mine. I looked around for the officer; he hadn't fired a shot, but was standing, some yards back in the corridor near the donkey and was clearly in a blue funk.

"They've got us cut off," he said, again loud enough that all could hear. "And have you seen them feed? And what they did to Jennings? We can't fight the likes of these. We're going to die here. We're all going to die."

His voice had been rising the whole time, and now echoed around the corridor. The donkey picked up on his panic and started to bray again. The sound of the beetles' drone outside got louder, more insistent.

"Shut that bloody thing up," Mac shouted. I wasn't sure whether he meant the donkey or the officer but there was certainly one of them I could deal with immediately. I slapped the young lieutenant, hard. He went quiet, a new red mark on his cheek accentuating his sudden paleness.

"I'll see you in chains and flogged for that," he said when he recovered his composure.

"Better that than in the belly of one of yon beasties," I replied. "Now be a good gentleman and keep quiet; you're frightening my lads."

He at least had the good sense to keep his mouth shut. He must have seen that I was more than ready to hit him again if it came to that. I turned my attention to the donkey, managing to calm it down without having to hit it; it clearly had more sense than our young C.O.

But I was too late. Mac shouted out from the barricades.

"Here they come again."

I got back to the men just in time to get them lined up properly again.

"Put that fag out, MacLeod. Eyes front, pick your targets. Remember, aim for the legs."

The moon had risen higher in the past ten minutes and now lit up the full length of the valley floor. I had a good, too good, view of the throng of beasts rallied against us. They seemed to cover the whole area in a seething black carpet, the larger ones crawling over the smaller in their haste to be at us. I've stood in some tight spots in my years of service, but nothing had ever chilled me to the core so much as those few seconds before the shooting started.

We just had enough room for all of us to line up along the barricade. Lieutenant Timkins was still holding back in the tunnel, so I called Hynd and Benson forward.

"The Lieutenant has got out backs, haven't you, sir?" I said, and this time I made sure I said it loud enough for all to hear. The young officer still looked pale, terrified even, but he nodded in reply, and then I had to turn away, for I couldn't afford to waste any more time on him.

The beetles were nearly upon us.

"Fire at will!" I shouted, and the valley echoed and rang with the crack of Lee Enfield rifles. The first rank of beetles fell immediately but this time the pack behind did not stop, either already engorged on their previous feeding, or too intent on reaching us, I would never know which. I took the legs off a big bugger that must have been near twelve feet from pincers to rear end, and Mac took another that looked bigger still, but no matter how many we put down still more clambered over and among the fallen.

The air stank of powder and also acidic tang I realized must be coming from the dead beasts themselves. Their bodies were piling up in front of the barricade, with ever more pushing up behind them, but luckily for us the press of beetles against their own dead was creating almost as effective a barricade as the old tables. And I knew my squad could keep pumping fire into them for quite some time yet, as long as the shells held out.

Even as I had that thought the first call for ammo came down the line, then another.

"Lieutenant," I called out. "We need a box of shells over here right now."

I turned, expecting to see Timkins getting the long box off the donkey's back. Instead the corridor was empty, there was no sign of our lieutenant, nor of the donkey, and more importantly, we had no more ammo to hand.

"I'm out," Mac called from the barricade.

"Me too," shouted Benson, just as a large black beetle forced its way forward. Jock stabbed it in the eye with his bayonet, then sliced a leg from under it. It was a small victory, for another crowded in immediately to take its place, with more coming over the top from behind it. Jim Woods tried the same trick with his bayonet but was grabbed tight in a huge pincer and swept away out of sight before any of the rest of us could move. His screams were loud, but mercifully short lived.

"I'm out," another man shouted from the line.

The beetles were now forcing themselves against the overturned tables and we were being pushed back to avoid being swamped, back into the corridor. If we were pushed back all the way to where it opened out into the temple, we would then be overrun in seconds. I had few choices left. I emptied my revolver into a huge beast that was threatening to charge through our defenses all on its own, and gave the order.

"Fall back, quickly now. Back to the temple, and back to yon staircase. It's our only chance."

As a man, we turned and fled. I heard, but

didn't see, the old tables of our barricade being torn into so much kindling as the beetles came through after us. Then there was only the sound of our running footsteps on stone and the ever increasing howl and drone of the beetles as they forced their way over and around each other in their desire to flood into the temple.

The lieutenant was already on the staircase behind the statue, trying to coax the donkey up the narrow steps. He saw us coming across the temple floor and with a squeal like a startled child turned and ran, bounding up the steps with no seeming thought to the danger of falling. He was soon lost in the gloom above. I had no time to consider his treachery just then, I had to get the men organized before we were completely swamped. Luckily for us the donkey did not bolt with the lieutenant, and stood long enough to allow Mac to divest it of the ammo box.

"Fill your sporrans, lads," I called out as I tried to find the box of cartridges for my revolver. "Then up the stairs, sharpish."

That was my plan, the only one I had, but I soon saw it wasn't going to work. The beetles swarmed into the temple, pouring through the archway and quickly covering the whole floor, if we turned our backs on them we'd be taken immediately. Our only option was a retreat up the stairs, but not a full, running flight, we'd have to take it slowly, watching our backs the whole way.

And hope against hope that the buggers would give us the time to make some kind of an escape.

One thing I didn't have to worry about was the donkey; as soon as we got the ammo off its back it turned and fled up the stairs, following Timkins into the darkness above.

"Follow that donkey," Mac shouted, and got a dry laugh from the rest of us. Then the beetles were upon us, and our fight for survival really began.

As a man we backed away to the stairs and started up. I was among the first on the stairs, next to Mac, Benson and Hynd and the four of us did our best to provide covering fire for the poor chaps bringing up the rear. Having to fire over the heads of our men sorely hampered our effectiveness; we couldn't help them with the closest beetles, instead we could only hope to keep enough of them at bay so that the nearest could be dispatched.

It worked, for a time at least, with us four at the top dragging the ammo box up with us, step by agonizing step, dispensing shells and providing covering shots where we could. But one by one the chaps fighting below us started to succumb to the encroaching horde of black carapaces. Ally Dunlop fell when he was too occupied with a pincer heading for his face to notice the smaller beetle that scuttled below his defense. It took a swipe at his shin, opening a wound down to the bone that sent the man to his knee, then quickly under a squirming, ravenous pile of the beasts. Colin Campbell stepped into his place and lasted as we backed up half a dozen steps, but a big brute of a beetle, ten feet long or more, barreled its way through its brethren, up the staircase and launched itself straight at the man. He put a bullet in its left eye and sliced its legs away from under it with his bayonet but its momentum carried it forward. A huge pincer caught Campbell by his waist, and his struggles, and the weight of the beast itself, toppled them both off the steps and away down to the temple floor, now some ten yards below us. At least the man was dead before he hit the ground, for the feeding frenzy that followed was a terrible thing to behold.

After that we developed a strange kind of rhythm for several minutes, reloading, dragging the ammo, then volleying covering fire before starting the process all over again. Nim Asbury was now our last line of defense, he took to it with gusto. He'd dispensed with the Lee Enfield in preference for his service sword, which he used to great effect in slicing legs and popping eyeballs, all the while weaving and bobbing like a dancer, keeping himself just out of reach of advancing pincers. He was one of the strongest, fittest men in the squad, but even he weakened eventually. He mistimed a thrust; his sword stuck between adjoining plates of the closest attacker's carapace and was dragged from his grasp. A beetle caught him by the ankle, another took him around the thigh, and he too tumbled away out of view to the ground that was now thankfully lost from sight in gloom below.

Still we climbed, ever higher into the darkness. There was little light to aid us from the temple below. When I chanced a look upward it was only to see a sheet of black, whether it was rock or merely a clouded sky I could not tell. In truth, it scarcely mattered, for it looked like we would be taken long before we reached the end of the staircase. The last two men, Smith and Henderson, both fell within minutes of each other, until there was only Benson, Hynd, Mac and me standing.

"I'm right sorry to have got you lads killed," I said as I shot out the front legs of the nearest attacking beetle. Mac leaned over my shoulder and speared the beast through the right eye, before sending it tumbling away with a push.

"Dinna talk shite, man," he said, edging past me to take what should have been my place at the rear. "We're no' done yet." He put a bullet into the head of a huge beetle, an instant before it was set to lop off his head. Then, dropping the rifle at his feet, he stepped forward and swung his backpack at the thing. I heard the pipes inside the pack squeal, and the beetles below us, as if in reply, answer with a louder drone of their own. The huge beetle Mac had shot wavered, and I thought it might tumble over. Then it steadied, and pushed forward. Mac planted his legs firmly against the join of step and rock and pushed back, grabbing its front legs and holding the beast high and away from his body. Its bulk covered the staircase, blocking any access from below. Mac had effectively created a new barricade, one that would only hold as long as he had his strength.

"Now, awa' ye go, man," Mac said. His muscles were bunched tight, and the strain showed in every feature, but he managed a grin, his teeth showing too white in the dark. "Get up the stairs. If yon wee jobbie Timkins is nae here, he must have got out. Go find him and give him a kick up the arse for me and the lads."

Even then I might have stayed, but Benson and Hynd dragged me away, and put themselves below me on the staircase. They stood over the remaining ammo in the box, loading their weapons. I took the chance to reload my revolver with the last six cartridges I had in my sporran and moved to cover them, but they too pushed me away.

"Do what Mac said, Sarge," Benson said. "We'll watch the big man's back for ye."

Hynd spat out a wad of chewing tobacco.

"Aye, get yerself gone, Sarge," he said. "We're right ahin ye. Somebody's got to get out of this mess, how will they ken who to give the medals to if we're all killed here?"

Mac shouted.

"Stop bloody arguing about it, just fuck off the lot of ye." His legs slipped, then he caught his grip again, but I saw he was weakening.

"I'll see you all up top," I said. "And that's a bloody order."

"Aye, right you are, Sarge," Benson said, moving behind Mac on the stairs. Hynd moved to stand next in line.

"Tell your wife I love her," Hynd said, winked, then turned his back on me.

I turned so that they would not see my tears, and ran, full pelt, up the empty staircase.

I didn't turn, didn't look back, so didn't see them fall, but I heard well enough; I heard the Lee Enfields crack and whistle, I heard Mac bellow and cry, heard his defiant shout of 'Fuck off, bastards,' then a last howl of pain. Hynd and Benson's guns fell quiet seconds later, and no matter how much I strained, I heard no more.

-DAVIES-

The captain and Wiggo were still poring over something on the laptop. Davies and Wiggo stood in the doorway smoking.

"Stay here and watch my back," Davies said. "I'll have a reccy out across yon plain; I don't like the idea of something sneaking across there without us being able to see it."

Davies made his way out to the main entrance and stopped, gazing in amazement at what had minutes before been a flat plain. Now it was liberally studded with dark oval shapes that he at first took for boulders, then had to re-evaluate when he spotted that several of them were most definitely moving.

"Cap, Sarge," he shouted. "You need to see this."

The sound of his voice caused a chain reaction of movement out on the plain. First the closer boulders moved, then it rippled out to the others until all of them were shifting and turning, as if focussing on Davies' position. Then the nearest, less than twenty yards away, rose up, six legs showing beneath a raised carapace. A squat head carrying two wicked pincers showed, rose and looked directly at Davies. The now well-known drone filled the air, taken up by firstly the closer of the beasts, then out across the plain until the canyon filled with the high, almost metallic, wail.

The first beast came forward, a giant black

beetle some eight feet long from pincers to tail end and almost four feet tall at the highest point of its shell. The carapace gleamed, a rainbow of glimmering color as the squat legs propelled it at surprising speed. Behind it more of the beasts were rising up from the ground, heads swivelling to gaze at the doorway.

Davies got his weapon up, took aim, and fired all in one movement, three quick shots into the tallest part of the first beast's back. Three puncture holes burst out a black, tarry ichor, but the thing didn't slow. He had to back away fast, still firing, three more holes in it and it kept coming. Davies backed away until he came up against the wall opposite the entrance to the temple area. The rest of the squad stood in the doorway there. But he couldn't chance stepping across to join them; the beast was still coming; it was almost on him.

"Aim for its legs," the captain shouted. "Legs or head, it's the only way to stop them."

The captain took his own advice and took out the attacking beast's front legs with a volley. Davies provided the coup-de-grace by blasting its head into fragments.

"To me," the captain shouted at him, but Davies didn't get time to respond; three more of the beasts clambered over the dead shell of the first, filling the passageway and cutting off Davies' path to the rest of the squad. Out on the plain a horde of beetles swarmed forward in a frenzied rush. The whole squad was shooting now, the archway full of ringing volley fire and the wail of the attacking beasts.

"I can't get across to you," Davies shouted after taking out the front legs of a creature only a foot from the end of his barrel.

"Fall back into the city," the captain shouted back. "We'll meet higher up. Go now; we can't hold this position."

Davies turned and ran, heading higher up a sloping causeway that led into the dark shadows of the city. Behind him the ringing gunfire continued before fading and becoming more distant as the rest of the squad backed away into the confines of the temple. He heard a muffled bang that sounded like the blast of a grenade but soon the sheer volume of stone around him muffled all sound save for the pad of his own feet...and the scuttle and scrape of insectoid legs on rock as the beasts came after him.

He tried not to think of the sheer number of beetles he'd seen out on the open plain. There had been scores of them, ranging in size from some no bigger than a man to others the size, and approximate shape, of the motorcars that shared their name. But his mind's eye betrayed him, showing him images of them filling up the passageways behind him, crawling over and around each other, droning and wailing as they followed him up through the city.

So far he'd been following the main route upward, a wide street that wound its way through the city, lined with what might have been commercial properties in some ancient past, and with long narrow alleyways running off towards the canyon walls on either side. Davies was strongly reminded of the vennels and closes in the old town in Edinburgh, but he doubted whether any of these would hide a welcoming pub or eating place to give him sanctuary.

But narrow might be better than wide?

At least in a narrow space he could get them one on one and have less chance of being overrun. Decision made, he took the first alley on his left, judging that direction to be the one that might have the best chance of meeting up with the squad's possible escape routes out of the temple below. It led him onto a staircase. He took the steps two at a time then turned when he heard loud scrambling and scratching on stone behind him.

A large beetle specimen had tried to follow him up the alley and proved to be too wide for the job. Its bulk now blocked the entranceway. Davies shot away its front legs then blew its head apart. It was so tightly wedged it barely slumped in death. A second beast clambered over the top of the wedged shell. Davies treated it the same as the first; legs then head spattering black ichor. It fell on the first one, effectively blocking the alleyway. Frantic scrabbling could be heard on the other side, the mass of beasts having been blocked from their prey. Davies wasn't about to hang around to see how long it took to clear.

He turned to the steps and fled up the shadowed alleyway.

Once again he was reminded of Edinburgh as he emerged at the top of a long winding flight of narrow steps onto a wider concourse built into the

canyon wall some thirty yards above the valley
floor. To his right a high parapet looked over the
lower reaches of the city, to his left on the other
side of the concourse it was a line of dwellings
built into the main canyon wall, a series of regular
rectangular doorways and square windows spaced
with rigid geometric regularity. There was no sign
that any of the beetles had made it up to this level.

Not yet anyway.

He stepped to his right and chanced a look
over the parapet. The main thoroughfare was fifty
feet or more below him and from directly below all
the way down the steep walled alley to the main
gate was filled by a swarming mass of the black-
shelled beetles. Their drone filled the air with its
harsh, almost electronic, wail.

An answering drone, louder still, came from
somewhere above Davies, higher up the valley. As
one, the beetles turned towards this new sound.
Davies was looking directly into a myriad of eyes
as they swivelled and found him.

The mad scrabble below intensified as if the
sight of him had enraged them.

Davies turned away and broke into a run.

He was heading upward and realised it might
be taking him closer to the source of that newer
drone. But the captain would expect him to be high
in the city. Behind him the droning rose again and
he didn't have to see it to imagine the beetles
pulling the blockage aside and pouring in a flood
up the alleyway in search of him.

He put on a burst of speed.

-BANKS-

Banks watched Davies flee into the city then directed the others.

"Back to the temple entrance," he said. "Let's see if we can keep their attention off Davies to give him enough time to get free."

They stood in a line, retreating step by step and firing until they reached the temple entrance.

"Stand firm here, lads," he shouted. "Give them hell."

The entranceway rang with gunfire. Bits of leg, fragments of black pincer and chunks of shell flew as the bullets ravaged the clambering beasts. A sliver as sharp as any piece of glass tore a path along Banks' cheek and blood flew. That enraged the attacking beetles even more and they pressed forward, a solid wall now floor to ceiling of scrambling, wailing frenzy. Wiggo had to step back to reload and the consequent press of the beast's attack was enough to force the three men back a step, then another. It wasn't going to be too long until they were forced back into the temple itself.

And once there we'll be overrun in seconds.

When it came his turn to step back to reload, he reached instead for one of the four L109A1 grenades he carried in his jacket.

"Fire in the hole," he shouted, pulled the pin and lobbed the grenade into the mass of the beasts.

"Leg it, to the stairs," he shouted. He deliberately slowed his own escape to allow Wiggo and Wilkins to get away first, and almost didn't get enough distance between himself and the bang, feeling the force of it at his back and the thunder of it in his ears. Ahead of him, Wiggo reached the foot of the stairs and turned. He had one of his grenades in hand.

"To me, Cap," the sergeant shouted and as soon as Banks reached the bottom step the grenade was lobbed over his head back towards the entranceway.

The three men were already on the stairs heading up when it went off with a bang that rang through the temple.

They went up two dozen steps before Banks chanced a look back. The entranceway swarmed with the beasts. Many had paused to feast on the remains of their dead that the grenades had blasted into a mess of broken shell and black ichor but others had already entered the temple and were coming forward towards the stairway.

"Do we stand, Cap?" Wiggo asked.

"Nope. You read how that worked out for the other squad back then. Leg it, all the way up. Somebody got out of this mess once before. If he did it, so can we."

Banks stopped again on the first main landing some forty feet above the temple floor, a floor that was now almost totally covered by beetles in a wide variety of sizes from no bigger than a small dog to monsters the size of pickup trucks. He saw them swarming around the dead bodies, both modern and old. They did not disturb the dead, moving through and around them almost as if in reverence to the huge statue that towered over them. Banks said a silent prayer against the desecration he was about to perform, took out two more of his grenades, pulled the pins and lobbed them down onto the valley floor. They landed directly at the base of the statue, under the head of one of the biggest of the beetles.

The resultant blast shook the temple and left a stunned silence in its wake. The big beetle that had been there was gone, bits of it strewn all across the floor, the bodies and other beetles, who had stopped droning and had turned their attention on the great black statue.

A loud crack, loud as any of their gunshots, rang out, then another as the statue wobbled to its right, appeared to right itself, then toppled, face down with a crash, directly on top of several of the bodies, squashing several more of the beetles in the process as the statue fell apart into half a dozen pieces. Another second of silence followed, then as one, the beetles took up their high, wailing drone again and the attention of every beast on the temple floor, in the entranceway and on the stairs below them turned to gaze directly at Banks.

"Give that man a coconut," Wiggo said. "Well done, Cap. You definitely got their attention. Now what?"

Banks didn't answer, just motioned that they should keep heading up. The swarm was heading for the stairs at their back as he went up the steps two at a time. This time he didn't look back, afraid to see what the beetles might be doing to the dead now that the idol had fallen.

They stopped on another high landing, a hundred feet above the temple floor, and more than halfway to the top. Beneath them the beetles reached the first landing and came on fast, scuttling and crawling over each other in their frenzy.

This time Wiggo and Wilkins did the honors, each of them lobbing a grenade down into the squirming mass. The blast, then resultant pause as the beetles scavenged their own dead, gave the three men enough time to gain several more paces on the chasing pack.

Banks was trying not to think of the fate of the last squad to take on this flight, or to wonder at each landing which of the Victorian soldiers might have chosen it as their last stand to protect their brethren. He focussed his mind on the stairs ahead, two at a time, no farther thought than the next step. It was a few seconds before he realised they were slowing; young Wilkins was in the lead, and had developed a limping gait, taking the stairs like a careful old man.

"It's the old wound, Sarge," he heard the private say to Wiggo. "Still gives me gip on stairs; I'm fine on the flat, but this is a right bugger."

"Dinna fash, lad," Wiggo said. "We've got your back. Get on up. We're right behind you."

Inadvertently or not, Wiggo had echoed the words from the earlier story, and Banks felt a chill up his spine as he joined the sergeant in turning on the next landing and looking down on the advancing horde below.

"Don't worry, Cap," Wiggo said. "Naebody's getting dead here today."

"I wish I had your confidence."

"Nah, you wish you had my tadger; go on, admit it."

Wiggo already had another grenade at the ready.

"I've got four more after this one," he said.

"I've got one left that I'd rather hold for an emergency," Banks replied.

"Fucking hell, Cap? If this isnae an emergency I'd hate to see what is."

The beetles were only twenty steps below, three abreast and packed tight on the stairs. Wiggo's grenade took out the front rank and Banks' rifle fire shot the front legs away from those that tried to follow, creating a temporary barrier where the pair of them were able to stand firm and take out any beetle that managed to scramble over.

The rearguard action had to be abandoned when a huge specimen barreled forward, its bulk sweeping the debris of the dead beasts off the stairs and down to the temple floor. Banks took out its legs, hoping to drop it in place as a new barrier, but the beast had enough life left in it to stagger aside before toppling off and falling away, clearing the path for the horde behind to launch a fresh attack.

Banks turned to see that Wilkins was almost at the top of the staircase above them.

"Last one up gets the beers in," he said and was off and running before Wiggo could react.

The beetles' drone rose in intensity; with their quarry in plain sight, they came up the stairs, a seething black train of fury.

-DAVIES-

Davies took another alley to his left that led into a narrow vennel even steeper than the first. He stopped twenty steps up, sure he had heard more muffled bangs in the distance, but the sound wasn't repeated. He turned and looked back down the alley; there was no sign as yet that he was being followed but he felt the chase at his back and was again reminded of his youth, fleeing amid the tower blocks of flats in Glasgow's East End with an angry mob after him for no other reason than he existed in what they considered to be their space.

Well, this time I've got a gun. Come and get it, bitches.

He ascended with no other thought than to reach the top, no goal but to reunite with the rest of the squad. This particular alley had dwellings, smaller but no less regular doors and windows spaced up its length, but they would have been dark places in which to live, never seeing the sun, lying constantly in deep shadow and carrying a chill despite the heat of the day beyond the canyon.

Fatigue was slowly taking a grip on him; it had been a while, what felt like an eternity, since either sleep or food. His training told him there was some more still in the tank; but not too much more. He reached the top of the alleyway and looked out over another open concourse, a narrower one this time. He turned to his right and looked up the canyon in dismay; the city rose up and away from him in a dizzying array of alleyways and streets, turrets and balconies.

He still had a lot of climbing ahead of him and wasn't sure he had the legs for it.

After one more upwards alley, one more long flight of steps, Davies' legs finally decided they'd had enough and developed a wobble that threatened to topple him backwards to probable broken bones or a cracked skull. He needed rest.

Finding a defensible position proved trickier than he'd hoped but in the end he chose a chamber high in a turret with a balcony giving a view over the lower end of the city. There was only one narrow entrance up a winding stairway; the larger specimens of the beetles wouldn't be able to negotiate it and he felt confident his rifle would be enough for anything smaller that might seek him out. The high vantage would also allow him to keep an eye open for the rest of the squad. All in all, it was the best he could hope for. Before declaring himself settled, he looked out over the balcony. The drop was sheer and straight from his position, fifty feet down to what looked to have been a marketplace at one time. Now it was empty save for stone and dust; there was no sign of the beetles in this part of the city and the fact that he hadn't been in sight of one for a good half hour gave him hope that they'd given up the chase.

He sat gratefully with a sigh of contentment to be finally off his feet, with his back to the balcony balustrade, keeping a close eye on the door to the stairwell while he had some water, a cold meal from his rations and a most welcome smoke. By the time he was done he was starting to feel better in himself but cold panic at his circumstances was always bubbling just under the surface now that the adrenaline rush of the fight then chase was wearing off.

He wondered how the others were getting on. He hadn't heard any gunfire, nor grenade blasts, but that might just mean that they too were hiding out and resting up. He could only hope that would be the case for the thought that they'd been overcome and that he was alone now in this vast empty city would be too much to take.

What with the reminders of Edinburgh, and thoughts of youthful flights from the gangs in Glasgow, his mind kept churning, past misery overlaying present circumstance, all jumbled together until the beetles became doped up youths and the city in the valley melded with the Scottish cities into an amalgam of almost medieval turrets and balconies with modern tower block lighting and windows and Davies' exhaustion finally wouldn't allow him to stay awake for a single moment longer.

He slept.

His dreams were troubled ones. He was back in Glasgow, back in his twelve-year-old body, hiding in a tower block stairwell while his tormentors prowled outside. It wasn't a new dream to him; he knew the beat and rhythm of it well enough from its recurrences over the years, but it never lost its power to unnerve him. He shivered there in the dark, for although he slept in the sun, here in Glasgow it was January, and deep in winter's grip.

Earlier that day the leader of the gang had got him on his own in a stairwell. That had been the lad's first mistake, but it had been enough to get him a broken nose and a blackened eye; Davies had been done messing around with the wankers. They'd been taunting him for months, blackie this and nignog that, their gang mentality giving baser instincts free rein in lieu of something better to do in the stairwells. The two punches that Davies threw had been his first ever retaliation; he knew his mother would give him hell for stooping to their level but, bloody hell, it had felt good.

He was paying for it now though; the lad was back from a hospital trip, acolytes gathered around him and the chase was on. So far it had taken them up and down three different blocks of flats; Davies was lucky in that he knew the passageways and stairwells just as well as his pursuers. But they'd almost caught him on the last flight and he'd had to jump over a rail to escape. The drop was higher than he'd have wanted, and he turned his ankle on landing.

Now all he could do was hide, and hope they wouldn't find him, for if they did, he didn't fancy his odds of staying out of hospital, or maybe even a coffin.

Cold gripped harder; he felt it seeping through his clothes at his back where he was pressed against a wall. He fought to stop his teeth chattering.

"Hey, Blackie," his main tormentor shouted from somewhere close. "Give us a smile so we can see you in the dark."

The only consolation Davies could take was that the lad spoke with a definite slur, courtesy of the newly wounded nose. Davies did indeed smile there in the dark, but it was a grim, tight-lipped one.

He shifted position as he heard them close in on him, pressing himself down into the darkest corner between two rubbish skips; the smell of discarded and rotted fast food was acrid, almost choking, but he was hoping that in itself would be enough to keep them from looking here for him. It wasn't that much of a hope in truth, for he knew from bitter experience that this lot would go a long way out of their way for any chance to torment him.

All he could do was crouch there in the dark and wait, hoping all the time that he could be somewhere else, somewhere he could see sunlight without fearing the exposure it lent.

Instinct woke him some time later, blinking confused for an instant by the brightness and heat in his hiding place, reality slowly creeping in around the remnants of the dream. He had no idea how long he'd slept, only that he didn't feel rested and that the sun was still high in the sky. None of that mattered in the face of the sounds coming from beyond the dark doorway ahead of him. Taloned legs scrambled and scratched on stone, clicking and clattering. A high droning wail rose up to wash over the balcony. Davies raised his rifle and pointed it at the doorway.

"Sarge, if that's you playing silly buggers I'm going to shoot you just for the hell of it."

It wasn't Wiggo. The beetle that came out of the shadows was no larger than a small dog and Davies almost laughed in relief. The wee bugger was fast though, he had to give it that, and he barely had time to pull his trigger and blow it apart with two rounds before it reached his feet. He reached down, scooped up the dead thing and lobbed it over the balcony, taking care to avoid touching the sickly black ichor that oozed from where its head had been. As the sound of the echoing gunfire faded and died around the canyon, he realised he'd just made a mistake, possibly a fatal one.

The only thing he had going for him was that the stairs up to his position were narrow, so he'd only have relatively smaller beasts to deal with. He stood, groaning as his legs and back rebelled, and moved inside the doorway to stand at the head of the stairwell. Now he had two things going for him; he also controlled the higher ground. But renewed scrambling and scratching down below him told him that the beetles must be aware of his position and it was only a matter of time before he had company.

He was trapped, no way out save over the balcony, with a limited supply of ammo and no backup.

The scuttling of talons on stone got louder, closer and a high wailing drone rose up from the dark stairwell.

Any time now would be fine by me, lads. Any time now.

-BANKS-

They fled up the stairs towards where Wilkins waited above, into the dark, imagining the black bodies of the beasts of hell at their back, thinking at any second to be plucked away into a death of a thousand cuts. Any daylight that made its way into the temple floor far below was thin and diffuse up here and they ascended into increasing darkness and shadow.

When they reached Wilkins' position Banks felt cold fresh air on his face, and saw, for the first time in long seconds, a hint, a merest glimmer, of light ahead.

"This way, lads," he shouted, and ran full pelt towards the light.

He reached a rock wall within five yards and saw light beyond a narrow cleft ahead. He forced himself into it, having to turn side on to pass through. For a horrible second he thought he might get stuck; if he'd had a beer gut he might be there yet, but with some degree of straining he was able to finally push through onto a wide open cliff-top ledge under blazing sun looking out over desert dunes far below.

Wiggo and Wilkins emerged at his side seconds later. They stood back, weapons raised but despite some frantic scrambling and scratching from the far side, none of the beetles made it through.

"Looks like this is how the old soldier must

have got out," Banks said.

"Aye, I think you could say that," Wiggo said dryly. "You need to see this, Cap. Wilko, watch our backs."

Banks turned to Wiggo to see him look down at a desiccated body sitting against the canyon wall to one side of the crack they'd just come through. It wore the red serge of a Victorian soldier, but obviously wasn't the one who'd written the journal. Banks knew immediately who this must be. He had a bullet hole between his eyes and a hastily scribbled note tucked into his tunic. Banks took it out and read it aloud.

"For desertion and abandoning his command in the face of the enemy. The sentence is death."

"Now we know why the auld lad didn't live off the story in his dotage back home," Banks said.

"He shot his C.O.?"

"Aye, and I'd probably have done the same in his place, but don't go getting any ideas, Sarge."

"So the auld lad made it this far. Then what?"

They studied the ledge and quickly found their answer. A precarious cliff track wound away down below them to where the cliff met the desert. Way off on the horizon to the east, Banks saw a darker patch of land that could only be the oasis. On the other side of the ledge an equally steep track led farther up the canyon. Banks realised that he was near to dropping; such a climb was out of the question without some rest, and looking at Wiggo and Wilkins he saw the same tiredness in their features that he felt in himself.

"There's our escape route," he said, pointing

down the cliff, "but first we find Davies. We told him to go high, so we'll be heading up. But not until we rest up."

Wiggo looked like he wanted to complain but Banks stopped him with a raised hand and pointed to the cliff.

"Be my guest, Sarge. But that's our way up, and yon's a perilous track. If your legs are anything like mine they won't take you very far before you fall off. It's a long way down."

Wiggo finally saw sense. Banks kept watch on the thin crack they'd come through while the sergeant and Wilkins got a brew of coffee going.

"Davies is a smart lad," Banks said when Wiggo handed him a mug. "He'll find a place to hunker down until we can get to him."

"It's a big city, Cap," Wiggo said.

"Aye, but you ken what the Scottish are like. We can find a countryman or a bar in any city in the world."

"If I get a vote, I'll settle for both."

There was no recurrence of the scrambling from beyond the crack in the cliff wall that led to the temple but Banks felt exposed out in the open on the ledge. He sent the others to a patch of shade that was developing near the upward cliff path as the sun passed over the top of the hill and put himself on first watch while they tried to catch forty winks. He stood with his back against the cliff face, alert for any sound behind him, smoking a succession of cigarettes and looking out over the desert.

He felt just about as tired as he'd ever been, and although they'd each eaten some field rations with their coffee, he knew it wasn't really enough to replace the energy they'd been expending since first finding trouble at the oasis. That felt like a thousand miles and a lifetime ago already.

And we've still got all the way back to go to get safe.

He pushed that thought away. The rescue was a busted flush but he had a different priority now; he had a man separated from the squad and in danger. Davies was all that mattered.

To try to turn his mind to other matters he looked again at the dried out body sitting against the cliff face. He had no pity for the dead man; being left to sit alone on a remote cliff ledge with no one to know his fate was no more than he deserved. He'd committed the cardinal sin in Banks' mind. He'd abandoned his squad at the time of their greatest need. Banks meant what he'd said to Wiggo, he would have given the officer the same fate had he been there back then, and walked away without a qualm. The squad was his life; to let them down was the greatest sin he could imagine.

He fell into the half-watching, half-asleep reverie again, looking out towards the oasis but seeing old campaigns in his mind, from Baffin Bay to Antarctica, from Siberia to the Amazon and across other deserts in Syria and Mongolia. And now here. Would he too end up on some forgotten clifftop when, as was probably inevitable, something finally caught up with them?

He made a vow to himself that, if that ever

happened, he'd ensure the squad was free and safe before he let anything take him and, standing there on that high ledge, he threw his promise out to whoever or whatever gods might be listening.

Wilkins spelled him after two hours and three and a bit hours later he woke, not quite refreshed but at least rested well enough that he felt that the climb might be possible. He had a coffee and a smoke with the others then turned his attention to the cliff path. Now that this side of the mountain was in shadow it looked even more dangerous and forbidding than before, but at least they'd be ascending away from the full heat of the sun. That was one of the few plus points.

But Davies has been up there for a long time alone now. Time we were going.

Five minutes later they were on their way.

Banks took the lead as they began their ascent.

-DAVIES-

Davies had been sleeping again, standing upright in the doorway leaning against the wall. He had no idea how long he'd been out, only that the sun had passed across above and was now starting its descent above the high end of the city.

You stupid bugger. You could have gotten yourself eaten.

There was no sound from down in the stairwell, no indication that any beetle had climbed up to take advantage of his lapse. And the sleep had done him some good after all; he felt rested now and, after a smoke and some chocolate from his vest, he felt alert.

But where are the lads?

He hadn't heard any gunfire since his initial flight and once again the old fear of being trapped and alone bubbled to the surface. He pushed it away angrily. Fear was of no use to him here. To try to counter it he took inventory; he had his rifle with two spare mags in his vest, he had a handgun with a full clip and four grenades slung at his belt. Not enough to take on an army but it should be plenty to keep him alive until backup arrived.

If it ever comes.

He pushed the thought away again and, to take his mind off it stepped over to look over the balcony to the city below. The streets lay in shadow now that the sun had passed, shifting darkness that obscured doorways and alleyways in impenetrable darkness. There could be any number of beetles down there, and he'd never know until he stepped into their midst.

He resolved to stay in place and wait, but the more darkness gathered the more he doubted his strategy. Had he come high enough? How would the others find him if he stayed quiet and hiding? As the sun went down over the highest part of the city and his position was thrown into shadow, he decided to stop second guessing himself and do something about it.

I need to get out of here. I need to get higher.

He stepped through the doorway, switched on his gun light and took his first step down the stairwell.

He immediately regretted his decision and almost stepped back onto the balcony but part of him was still back in his dream, still cowering between rubbish bins at the base of a tower block in Easterhouse. Stepping back now would be like admitting he was still the scared lad, hiding in the dark. His tormentors in Easterhouse would have thought twice about taking on the man who smiled grimly, grabbed his rifle tight, and took a second step.

He took the steps slowly, taking care not to make a sound, not even a scrape of shoe on stone. The stairwell wound down and around the interior of the turret so he could never see more than a few feet ahead of him at any point but there was no hint that the beasts were anywhere close, no droning, no scramble of talons on rock and no trace of the acrid odor he'd come to associate with them. His confidence grew with every safe step downward but was quickly shattered on reaching the foot of the stairwell.

He looked out over the market area he'd seen from above. The air was still and quiet and the marketplace was cast in deep shadow now, but not too deep to hide the almost hemispherical domes that littered the whole area in sizes varying from man-sized up to several as big as automobiles. None were paying attention to him; all had their legs and heads pulled in and shells resting on the stony ground. But the alley he needed to take was off to his right and in order to get higher in the city Davies was going to have to walk among at least some of the beasts without them noticing him.

His first thought was to retreat back up the stairwell to the balcony, but the decisions he'd made to come down from there still applied. He had to get higher, that was the single greatest imperative. Okay, there were beasties in his way. But they hadn't seen him yet. Once again he brought to mind his time in Glasgow; he'd evaded tormentors through stealth and cunning back then and those guys, while being none too smart, certainly had the beating of these beetles when it came to conviction.

You can do this.

He took a step out into the marketplace.

Nothing stirred. The oval domes lay there like strategically placed sculptures in a modern art museum. Emboldened, Davies took another step, then another. He skirted one of the larger specimens, marvelling at the rainbow sheen of its shell and the sheer impression of brute strength its solidity gave off. He treaded carefully amid the creatures, moving slowly, almost in slo-mo, even when his every instinct was just to leg it and hope for the best.

He was halfway to his goal of the alley entrance when the nearest beast to him, a specimen almost seven feet long, stirred and raised its shell. A leg came out, only six inches from his foot and a long talon that looked almost metallic scratched at the stone with a shriek like fingernails on a blackboard.

Davies went still, as if playing a childhood game of statues, one foot raised mid-step, the other now only four inches from the scratching talon.

Three inches now, and the talon scratched again, harder this time, the resultant noise louder, more insistent. Several other of the shells stirred as if in response and that was Davies' signal to move. He threw caution to the wind and ran full tilt for the alleyway.

It was only ten yards but he almost didn't make it; one of the larger creatures blocked his way. He had to make a quick decision: go round or go over. Over was faster. He leapt onto the thing's back. As soon as it took his weight it shifted, rising up and threatening to overbalance him but his momentum was just enough to keep him moving forward. As he leapt off and into the mouth of the alleyway the characteristic high wailing drone rose behind him. By the time he'd gone up three steps he heard scrambling and scratching on stone at his back. He turned, rifle raised, to see the creature he'd just vaulted stuck firm in the mouth of the alleyway.

He considered firing, decided that the noise might do more harm than good and left the beast scrambling there while he turned for the stairs. He looked back after he'd taken thirty of them; smaller beasts were now clambering over the large one and beginning a pursuit.

But I've got a head start. That's better than I could have hoped for.

He went up the flight of steps at a dead run, two at a time, another trick he'd learned young in the tower blocks.

He knew they were behind him. He could envision them packed shoulder to shoulder and legs to shells in a swarming mass coming up the alleyway like lava under force. He didn't turn to look, concentrating instead on speed and surefootedness on the steps. When he arrived at the top of the alleyway he was on another concourse, one that ran high along the canyon close to the upper rim. There were no dwellings here; it had a sense of being a viewing platform for the city below, like a visitor's area on a great dam. Over to the east, darkness was already engulfing the city while above him the highest ramparts still gleamed redly in the last of the sun.

Davies looked across the causeway, hoping for another alleyway to lead him to the tops. This time he was out of luck. The concourse stretched away to the right and left on either side of him. Across the way, at this point at least, there was only the rocky wall of the canyon. Going left meant heading back in the direction of the main city. Going right would at least keep him in twilight for the time being and there were high towers in that direction, the very topmost part of the city, still basking in the last of the sun, jutting up above the canyon wall like tombstone teeth.

He barely slowed, went right, and broke into a sprint.

He only turned a minute later when the high droning wail of the beasts took on an even higher pitch that sounded almost excited. He looked back over his shoulder and almost tripped over his feet; he had been found. The beasts were only fifty yards behind, a wall of them stretching across the concourse and filling with a black wave that rolled forward like a breaker in a high sea.

Davies set his gaze on the nearest of the high towers ahead; it was now his only hope in a race for safety.

It was going to be touch and go. Halfway to the tower he looked back again. The black wave was still coming, barely twenty-five yards behind now, close enough that he heard the scrape and scramble of talons on stone even above their insistent wailing drone. He tasted the acrid odor of them at the back of his throat. His breath came hard and heavy, his legs feeling as if they were on fire, and he knew that a single stumble would be the end of him; they would be onto him before he had time to rise. A black doorway at the base of the nearest tower became his single point of focus. It was thinking of Glasgow again that gave him a last spurt of energy; he hadn't let them catch him back then.

I'll be buggered if I'll be caught now.

He reached the doorway only yards ahead of the rushing horde and almost cried in relief when an open hallway led to a spiral stairwell similar to the one he'd used before. He went up two turns before taking a second to unhook a grenade from his belt. That moment's pause was almost fatal; one of the smaller beasts, two feet long but full of fury, snipped with a pincer and Davies felt it scrape bone at his ankle. There was wet heat as blood flowed in his boot.

Trusting that the structure had survived this long and would take the blast, Davies kicked the attacking beast away, pulled the pin between his teeth and lobbed the grenade down the stairwell. He saw it bounce away, he turned and bounded up the steps, two paces, then threw himself face down as a blast of heat and light washed around him.

His ears rang, the hair at the back of his head was singed, and he still felt blood pool in his left boot from the wound the beast had given him, but when he turned and looked back, the stairwell was full of smoke...and empty of beetles.

He made it up to the top of the stairs at a hobble, listening all the time for the scrape of talon on stone. The ringing in his ears slowly subsided, at the same time the pain in his ankle grew to a white-hot flare. He was almost at the limit when he saw dim light ahead and one circuit of the stairwell later brought him out onto a high balcony. Stars were beginning to twinkle into view to the east while to the west he looked down into what appeared to be a several miles wide crater; the valley emerged at this point onto an extinct volcano of an age that could only be guessed at. Davies had more important matters on his mind; his ankle was still bleeding, and in his already weakened state every ounce of blood was needed.

He sat with his back to the parapet, rolled up his trouser leg and eased off his left boot and sock. He saw bone gleam inside a three-inch gaping wound that was oozing blood. He set about patching himself up.

It was a fraught process, what with having to keep one eye on the stairwell while also performing some rudimentary stitchwork. The cut edges were razor straight, which helped with the needlework, and a shot, as small as he thought he could get away with, of morphine took the edge off the pain. He bandaged it up as tight as he could bear and put his sock and boot back on; he might not be able to manage that later if the wounded area swelled up. The morphine kicked in and took the pain down to a dull ache and after a smoke he felt almost in control.

For now.

But he wouldn't be doing any more running any time soon, that was for sure. It wouldn't take much pressure on the wound to open up his stitching, and that was before taking into account the pain that he knew was just waiting to reassert itself.

He sat there in the growing dark, nerves tingling, rifle pointed at the doorway, and waited to see if the beasts would find him. If that happened, he intended to take as many of the bastards with him as his ammo would allow.

-BANKS-

Banks heard the distinctive crack of a grenade going off just as darkness was falling across the face of the cliff.

"He's still alive," Wilkins shouted.

"Of course he fucking is," Wiggo said. "You think I'd climb this fucking hill for a dead man?"

The climb had been every bit as perilous and arduous as Banks had feared. They'd been on the narrow trail for two hours now, wending their slow way upward, on hands and knees in places where it got particularly steep. The sound of the blast lifted spirits that had been flagging and gave him a renewed burst of stamina; one of his men was up there, still fighting.

Banks had been in the lead for the whole climb to this point, the others taking their pace from him. When he put on a burst of speed, Wiggo was the first to complain.

"Steady on there, Cap. I'm no' a fucking goat."

"That's no' what the wifies of Lossiemouth say," Banks replied, and only got a tired laugh in reply. The sound of the grenade had him wanting to press on, but his body, and his men, could only take so much punishment at a time. He forced himself to take a rest; he called it a smoke break for form's sake but none of the three of them were fooled. They stood close together on a narrow ledge high above the desert. Off to the east, stars were appearing above the oasis, while the tops of the cliff, still some way above them, were fringed in red from the dying rays of the sun.

"It's going to be dark the rest of the way," he said.

"Have you no' got any good news, Cap?" Wiggo asked.

"It's not raining. And there's nae beasties about."

"Aye, thank fuck for small mercies. Maybe they've got better sense than to be climbing a bloody cliff at this time of night."

While they smoked, Banks was listening for another grenade or gunfire, more evidence that Davies was still fighting, but there was no repeat of the earlier noise and ten minutes later he could stand no more waiting.

He turned back to the cliff and climbed.

The ascent went on for what seemed like forever. Banks was aware that he was getting slower but the lads behind him weren't complaining so he guessed they were feeling it every bit as much as he was. It was almost a relief to come to what appeared to be an ancient rockfall area, a huge hollow area in the cliff that they'd have to skirt carefully around, but on a level section of track. It was only after they'd traversed a third of the rim of the hollow that Banks saw what filled it and that was only made possible by the light of a rising moon in the east.

He'd heard the stories of vast elephant's graveyards in Kenya; this must be something similar was his first thought. The hollow area, almost a hundred yards wide and cut deep into the cliff, was full of empty carapaces of dead beetles, some whole, some broken, some still containing parts of limbs and pincers, others oozing sickly ichor that looked jet-black in the moonlight. The whole place stank like a charnel house. Looking up the slope he thought he could see more discarded shell fragments littering the cliff face, all the way down from the tops to the hollow.

"They came over the side from way up there?" Wilkins asked.

"Looks like it, lad," Banks said. "Came, or were made to come."

Wiggo pointed at a shell the size of a small bus.

"What could put a thing like yon over a mountain top?"

"A bigger thing like yon," Banks said grimly. "But let's hope that's one wild guess I don't get right. Come on, lads. These are dead. Davies isn't."

They walked quickly around the charnel pit and Banks was almost glad when the trail climbed away from it and a breeze from the east meant that not just the sight, but the smell of the dead things was behind them. A quiet had fallen over the mountain and all he heard was the men's feet on the rock and his own breathing. Even Wiggo had fallen silent and they climbed that way for another half hour before Banks looked up to see the cliff top was definitely much closer; they were finally approaching their destination. He stopped the squad for another smoke break.

"Right, lads. We're nearly there. We don't ken what to expect once we get over the top, but Davies is up there somewhere, probably waiting for us, maybe in trouble. We find him, and we leg it out of here."

"Now there's a plan I can get behind," Wiggo said. "And what about yon dead researchers?"

"As you say, they're dead. It's not as if we can take them with us. Their final rest lies in the hands of the diplomats but if you ask me, they'll just quietly get forgotten. We were never here, nobody ever saw us, this place doesn't exist."

"Same as it ever was," Wiggo said and flicked the glowing butt of his cigarette away over the cliff into the night as Banks turned for the final stage of the climb.

They came to the top with the rising moon at their back. He hadn't known what to expect, but the sight surprised him nevertheless. They stood on a high ledge, looking west across what looked to be the vast crater of a long dead volcano. There was enough moonlight to see that the caldera had formed an oasis of foliage and glistening pools of water that danced in the moonlight. There were other shadows too, too dark to penetrate, but they looked to be natural rather than man-made. This spot was the very highest reach of the city.

Banks turned to look eastward. They stood thirty feet above a high wall that ran across to the other side of the valley. The wall was twenty feet thick and topped with a wide causeway that was cast deep in shadow. Turrets loomed even higher at regular intervals along the top, the highest points of each level with Banks' eye line as he stood up on the ledge; they too would have a view in daylight over the massive crater beyond. He searched in vain for any glimmer of light at the dark windows. If Davies was in one of the turrets, he was keeping his head down.

"Right, lads. I have no intention of blundering around the city in the dark; that's just asking for trouble we don't need. But I told Davies to get high, and yonder turrets are the highest things here. I'd like to check them out. If he's not there, we wait for him; if he is there, we secure a location and wait out the night. Either way, we get a rest."

"That sounds like another fine plan to me, Cap," Wiggo said. "What's first?"

Banks risked using the night light on his gun to strafe the immediate area and found what he was looking for; another track, or rather, a flight of stairs, leading down from their position to the high concourse.

"Well, at least it's not upward," Wiggo said, and took the lead on the stairs.

They descended into darkness with only moonlight and stars to show the way but Banks was loath to switch on their gun lights.

"No sense in giving away our position unnecessarily," he said quietly. "Easy does it, lads."

As they approached the causeway, he saw that he'd been right to be so circumspect; the flat area between where they stood and the doorway to the first turret was full of domed, dark shadows, none of them moving. Scores of the beetles, all with their legs and heads tucked in, like limpets on seaside rocks. Wiggo stopped at the foot of the stairs. The nearest beast was only ten paces away, a large one some ten feet in length, its dome six feet tall.

'What now, Cap?" Wiggo whispered.

"The plan's still the same," Banks replied. "We need to check out these turrets. We know they are triggered by sound. Let's make sure we don't make any."

He squeezed past Wiggo and took the lead again. They had good reason to be thankful for the moonlight; on a cloudy night they would have been forced into using their lights but as it was each of the black domes was clearly delineated against the lighter stone of the causeway. He went to the right of the first large beast and looked ahead, trying to see the easiest path they could take through the creatures. Wiggo and Wilkins came up behind him in single file, walking in his footsteps.

They inched forward, painfully slowly, carefully placing their feet on solid ground before attempting the next step. An acrid odor hung in the air and tickled Banks' throat, threatening a cough that he had to stifle but even then the resultant chuff in his throat sounded far too loud in the deathly silence on the causeway. He stopped mid-step but none of the creatures stirred. They skirted another huge beast, so tall in the dome that Banks couldn't see round it. Once clear of it he finally had a clear view of the turret doorway. The beasts were packed so tight around it there didn't appear to be any way through them.

It became a moot point seconds later. Two gunshots cracked from the turret high above. The moment's relief of the discovery that Davies was still alive was quickly forgotten as all around them the beasts stirred. Talons scraped on stone, domes rose off the ground, and heads emerged to investigate this latest noise. The high droning wail rose up all around the three men who were now trapped in the midst of the waking horde.

"Move!" Banks shouted. "Let's plough the road."

-DAVIES-

The attack had almost taken Davies off guard. He'd been checking his pockets for his cigarettes when he heard the scrape on the steps immediately outside the doorway ahead of him and barely managed to get his rifle aimed as a dog-sized beetle barreled through. It came straight for him; he put two bullets in its head but its momentum meant it kept coming and it fell on his feet and ankles, bringing a flare of pain to his wound and causing him to yell out.

That brought more scraping and scurrying on the stairs. He had another flashback to his youth in Glasgow, the wee frightened lad hiding in the dark. That time he'd been cowering, terrified.

But I'm not that lad anymore.

"Come and get me, if you think you've got the balls for it," he shouted.

In answer, he heard the ring of gunfire from the causeway below the balcony.

"About fucking time the cavalry got here," he shouted, then had to concentrate on his own survival as the scrape of talons on stone on the stairs got louder and the high wailing drone of the beetles echoed across the moonlit city.

The second beast to try its luck was bigger than the first, almost twice the size, but he had more time to prepare for it and put it down, front legs then head, in the center of the doorway, providing a ready made barrier that any other attack would have to clamber over. He considered lobbing a grenade over the top of it but he had no guarantee it would drop down the stairwell far enough to protect him from the blast and neither could he lob one over the parapet, for fear of killing one or more of the squad. Besides, it looked like he was going to be too busy with the rifle to bother with much else; a third beast came over the top of the dead one in the doorway. One round in each leg, one in the head, it was becoming a ritual, and the beetle fell atop its brother although it was much smaller and didn't add much to the barrier.

A grenade went off amid the roar of gunfire; it sounded as if it came from directly underneath him.

"Up here. I'm up here," he shouted, then had to defend himself again as a fourth beast came over the top of the others. This one was bigger still and must have had a struggle in the narrow stairwell. One in each leg and one in the head did for it and it too fell in the doorway. His barrier was now four feet high. There was frantic scrambling and frenzied high droning from beyond it. The sound of gunfire came up from somewhere down the stairwell.

Rescue was getting closer. All he had to do was stay alive long enough for them to get to him. But his chances weren't looking good. The barrier of dead beetles in the doorway moved as if pushed from behind, then shifted again, the whole thing coming six inches closer.

The uppermost of the dead beetles toppled sideward, leaving a gap that was quickly filled. Two smaller ones came through at once. He switched to rapid fire, put three rounds in the nearest one, blasting the whole thing to a stinking pulp, but didn't have time to aim at the second. It scuttled across the balcony floor, over his feet and ankles bringing a fresh white sear of pain in his wound, and was in his lap before he had time to react to it. A huge pincer tried to tear at his flak jacket; he didn't want to wait to see which of them won out. He dropped his rifle and grabbed the beast in both hands. The shell tore a gash in his left palm then he finally had a grip of it. He lifted it above his head. Legs squirmed and a pincer snapped shut an inch from his nose but by that time he had a firm hold. He tossed it backward over his head and it sailed away over the parapet.

If it hits Wiggo on the head there'll be hell to pay.

He retrieved his rifle just in time; another beast, almost as wide as the doorway, clambered its way over the dead. Davies aimed, fired... and came up empty. He ejected the mag and reached for a fresh one but knew it was just a last gesture of defiance; the beast would be on him before he got to slam the mag home.

-BANKS-

The fight across the causeway into the turret doorway and onto the stairs was already taking on the flickering shadowy semblance of a bad dream. The three men had almost been overrun in the first seconds and it was only Wiggo's smart thinking to make use of the high dome of the largest beast in the area to take the high ground that saved them.

"To me," the sergeant shouted, as he took out the legs and head of the massive beetle and climbed up onto the top of the shell. From there he began ploughing a furrow between them and the doorway to the turret. When Banks and Wilkins leapt up to join him the three of them joined in a rapid-fire volley that sent bits of shell and limbs and pincers flying in a mist of tarry black ichor. The ferocity of their assault seemed to give the beasts pause, and they stopped coming forward in quite so many numbers.

Banks saw a chance.

"Wiggo, lob a grenade towards the doorway, then, when I make a run for it, leg it after me. Don't be slow."

When the grenade went off, the beetles that weren't caught in the immediate blast scattered away from the area. Banks leapt down and ran for the vacant space, hoping that Wiggo and Wilkins were right behind him. He reached the turret doorway to find a large beetle facing him in the hallway. He took it down fast, legs and head and had to leap up and over it to get into the stairwell proper.

After that it was an interminable fight for territory up a dark stairwell, gun lights sweeping into shadowed areas, beetles making darting attacks from around bends, boots splashing in tacky oozing gloop as they climbed in a haze of stink, gunfire and the steady high wail of ever more frantic beetles. At one point he heard Wilkins shout out.

"Fire in the hole."

Three seconds later there was a muffled crump below them and then a quick blast of heat at their backs. Gunfire came down from above them. Davies was still alive, still fighting.

The battle for the stairwell went on. Banks' mag came up dry and he allowed Wiggo to squeeze past him while he reloaded. He watched for anything that might get past Wiggo's rapid fire and tried to avoid standing in any of the dead beetles they had to go over to go up.

Wiggo's mag went dry. When Banks moved to squeeze past him a beetle almost as wide as the stairwell launched itself full pelt down towards them. Banks put six rounds in it before it fell an inch from his toes, his bullets blowing holes in its shell and splashing stinking black gloop all across his chest and thighs. They had to climb over the creature before they got sound footing once again on the stairs.

Davies' gunfire was much closer now and when Banks took the next turn of the stairs, shooting two more dog-sized beasts in the back as he climbed, he saw dim moonlight ahead. He burst through the doorway in time to see a huge beast making straight for Davies, who was struggling to get a fresh mag into his weapon. Banks put six shots in the thing's arse, blowing its whole rear end to pulp but it didn't slow, crashing straight into Davies who was now hidden under its bulk.

"Wiggo, get in here, I need a hand."

The two of them caught the beast by the rear end, their hands covered in the black gore, and lifted and pushed at the same time. The beast went away over the parapet and they heard a crash as it hit the causeway below.

Sudden silence fell over the balcony. Banks looked down to see Davies smile up at him.

"You took your bloody time."

Wilkins spoke from the doorway.

"All quiet below, Cap," he said. "I think we gave them something to think about."

Banks sniffed at the mess of goo that coated his fingers.

"Aye, and they did the same for us."

He looked around at the sticky remains of dead beetles that coated the balcony.

"Let's send this lot to join their mate," he said. "And see if we can make this spot habitable, at least until sunup."

They spent ten minutes tossing beetles and bits of beetles over the balcony and made an attempt at getting rid of the worst of the gloop using one of Wiggo's spare shirts from his pack as a mop.

"I don't think this would pass the sniff test," Wiggo said, holding up a sodden, blackened mass of cloth. He tossed it away over the balcony.

By the time they had a stove on and a brew of coffee bubbling, the adrenaline rush of battle was fading and the ringing in Banks' ears no longer sounded like church bells tolling beside his head.

Davies brought them up to date with his adventures in the city and Wiggo told a lurid version of their own journey from temple to turret while they had a smoke and a coffee.

"What now, Cap?" Wiggo asked.

Banks addressed Davies first.

"How bad is the wound? Will you be able to walk on it?"

"I've bound it up tight and it hurts like blazes, but I should be fine, for a while anyway."

"We'll see how it is in the morning. Getting out of here is going to be hard enough in daylight; I'm not about to risk it at night. This is as good a position as any to defend, so we'll rest up here. Two hours watch each and we'll get gone at first light. I'll take first watch. Wiggo, take an inventory before you bed down; I've got a feeling we're going to need every bit of ammo we have left if we're going to get out of here."

Wiggo's inventory proved him right; they were down to a mag and a half of ammo each for the rifles. All of them had handguns with full clips and between them they had eleven grenades remaining. If they were going to get out of here, they'd need to use stealth more than force, given that the horde of beasts appeared to be almost limitless in number. To make matters worse they were running short of water; he estimated they'd have enough, if rationed, to get them back to the oasis and fresh supplies but it would be tight, and they'd have to leave as soon as they were all rested. Then they'd only have a horde of rabid giant beetles to contend with between them and safety.

"Where the fuck are they all coming from?" Wiggo asked as he and Banks shared a smoke in the doorway after Davies and Wilkins got their heads down. "And what do they eat out in in the middle of fucking nowhere?"

"We've already seen that they eat each other, in a push," Banks said. "But I'm sure they'd fancy a bit of us given half a chance."

"Do you think it was them that had away with all the people that used to live here?"

"I think that's probably more likely than not, don't you?"

"One thing's for sure, the beasties didn't build yon statue you destroyed. So what did we have here? Do you think they worshipped them? Beetlemania?"

Banks smiled thinly at that.

"Speculation gets us nowhere. Let's see what the morning brings. Get your head down; we're all shagged out and living on fumes."

After Wiggo finally bedded down, Banks stood looking over the moonlit city. It was strangely beautiful, ageless and solid under the stars. He knew that some of the darker shadows concealed more of the beetles but for now the beasts had returned to ignoring the men. If they were still quiet in the morning there was a chance the squad might be able to creep through them and make an escape.

He hoped that would be the case, for this was already a fucked-up rescue mission.

It couldn't get any worse, could it?

He was asleep a minute after Wilkins took over watch duties from him.

He woke with the dawn to see Davies and Wiggo standing at the balcony looking over the opposite view from that across the city.

"Fuck me sideways," Wiggo said.

Banks rose to join them. He was forced to agree with Wiggo's comment.

Last night they'd seen the huge crater from up on the lip but the night had hidden its secrets. Now, with the coming of day they were exposed. The ancient dead volcano stretched away for several miles below them. At the nearer end, below the causeway wall, there was a ledged platform containing what appeared to be an altar. Strewn around it, covering an area the size of a football ground, was a sea of bleached bone, all too human, long dead skulls grinning in the morning light. Beyond that, the crater was a natural oasis, a vast forested area punctuated with pools of water that appeared to steam in the daylight. Between these pools, on long used trackways, moved beetles, travelling in trails like an army of ants, but ants the size of horses, and many larger still.

There were thousands of them. They seemed to congregate tighter together in the center of the caldera over a mile away where Banks saw a black, domed hump, the unmistakable shape of a great beetle. He hoped it was dead, for it was the height of a house and seeing it move wasn't on his list of things to do for the day.

"Can we no' just call in a wee air strike, Cap?" Wiggo said. "Blast all these fuckers away at one time?"

"We're not even supposed to be here. You ken that. They're not about to let us provoke an international incident, or even a war, over the sake of a few beetles, no matter how fucking big they are. No. We get out of here, shank's pony, right fucking now, and we leave the big decisions to those that get paid to make them."

He went to the other side of the turret to check out the view below. He'd hoped to see a quiet scene of dormant beasts but the whole causeway was a seething mass of beetles. It took him several seconds to realise what he was looking at; they were scavenging their dead, eating the soft parts and carrying the shells and debris away. A steady train of beetles went over the side of the causeway and down into the caldera where they joined the file heading into the center, towards the large hump.

The only ones not in motion were the four beasts, each the size of a small car, who sat directly in front of the doorway that was the squad's only means of escape.

-DAVIES-

Davies joined the captain in looking down over the causeway. Standing had proved to be less of an effort than he'd feared and his bad ankle was bearing his weight just fine, for now at least, so he held off on the self-administered morphine in favor of a clear head.

"In coming to get me, you've managed to trap yourself here," he said.

"Aye. But we got to you, so I count it as a win," Banks replied. "How's the ankle?"

"Bearable. I doubt I'll be doing any five-minute miles though."

"Don't tempt fate, lad. We might have some running to do this day."

I bloody hope not.

The captain was still looking down at the four huge dormant beetles guarding the doorway.

"I've got a plan," he said. "But you're not going to like it."

Banks called the others over.

"I want you three to get down to the bottom but stay around the first bend above the main entrance."

"What about you, Cap?" Wiggo said.

"I'll be up here, lobbing two grenades down onto those four beasties," he said. "When they blow, you head for the foot of the stairs up to the rim. Then you cover me from there while I leg it down and across to join you. Just don't fucking shoot me."

As a plan its main benefit was its simplicity; there weren't too many parts to go wrong, but Davies knew it would all depend on speed. He could only hope his ankle stood up to it.

He was at the rear of the group of three going down the stairs five minutes later. The captain had synchronized his watch with Wiggo's but Davies had no means of checking the time; his own watch had stopped, broken at some point during the adventures of the night before. All he could do was follow Wiggo and Wilkins down the steps and hope that the captain and the sergeant had got their timing right. They came to a turn near the bottom, Wiggo went down four more steps then turned and motioned them backwards for four. He looked at his watch.

"One minute," he said softly.

A minute had never felt so long to Davies, then Wiggo held up three fingers, two, one, and right on cue there was a deafening crash from ahead and down in the entranceway.

"Leg it," Wiggo shouted, and took the lead without turning to check if he was being followed.

The immediate area in front of the doorway was a blasted jam of black ichor and bits of carapace. Davies splashed through it, all thought of a damaged ankle forgotten as adrenaline kicked in. All around them beetles had scattered after the grenade blasts but already heads were turning and talons scraped on rock as the now well-known high drone was taken up all along the causeway.

The first part of the captain's plan was successful enough; the three men reached the foot of the steps and turned, weapons in hand, already taking aim. Captain Banks appeared in the doorway of the turret but the brief respite provided by the grenades hadn't lasted; the beasts closed in on his position. Davies went to step forward to his aid but Wiggo held him back.

"Cap's got this," he said. "Cover his left flank. Wilkins, right flank. I've got his back."

The captain broke into a run while at the same time maintaining rapid fire from his rifle aimed directly ahead of him. Wiggo took out a large creature that attempted to come up behind the running man; there was no subtlety in it, no finesse of going for head or legs. Wiggo blew holes in its shell from just above its head along its back and kept firing until it went down. Davies chose a target that was moving in on the captain's left flank and, taking Wiggo's lead, kept firing until it went still.

Things were happening fast. Wiggo put down two small ones almost under the captain's feet, Davies concentrated on a large one that was just beginning to move, taking out its front legs as the shell lifted from the ground. The captain was only yards away now but a horde of twenty or more of the beasts were gathering ten paces behind him.

"Grenades," Wiggo shouted.

He, Wilkins and Davies all had a grenade in hand two seconds later.

"Fire in the hole," Wiggo shouted. All three men pulled their pins and threw at the same time. The pineapples fell amid the bunch of beetles and they went off in three distinct crumps, blasting a haze of vaporized shell and ichor across the concourse.

The cap arrived on the steps, breathing heavily, but he didn't stop, immediately heading up the stairs towards the crater rim.

Davies followed at his back, aware as he took to the stairs that his ankle was hurting.

They went up the staircase to the rim at a flat run and Davies was out of breath when they reached the top. The captain didn't pause but turned away onto an outer cliff path that threaded down the outer wall of the mountain towards the desert far below. Davies paused for several seconds to catch his breath before following. He happened to be facing into the long caldera. A movement caught his eye at the center. A vast mass of beetles was on the move, heading towards the city. The high black dome of the massive beetle rose up, a head the size of a cow emerged and even at that distance, Davies seemed to feel a malevolent glare that was directed straight at the squad.

"It's coming," he said.

"Aye, and so's Christmas," Wiggo said at his back. "Get a fucking move on, son. We hivnae got all day."

Davies turned to follow the captain.

His ankle was definitely hurting more now, and as he descended, he developed a noticeable limp from the flare of pain that came with every step.

-BANKS-

Banks took the lead all the way down to the beetle burial pit they'd seen earlier. He stopped there to look back up the trail.

There was no sign of pursuit, which was just as well. Davies was slowing the others' descent, obviously hampered by the wound in his ankle. The private saw Banks looking higher up the cliff.

"Are they after us, Cap?"

"No. Not yet at least," Banks replied. "Take it easy along this flat stretch. If there's still no pursuit, we'll take a rest at the high ledge; that's about halfway down by my reckoning. Are you okay for that?"

Davies gave him a thumbs-up. Banks saw the pain etched on the younger man's features, but said nothing; there was an unwritten rule among them. If one of the squad said they were okay, you believed them until proved wrong; he owed it to the men to give them the opportunity to test their limits. Davies had come through adversity before, he had to be trusted to do so again.

Banks waited until Wiggo and Wilkins had caught them up then continued along beside the charnel pit. He kept a wary eye on the cliff tops high above, but still there was no pursuit.

He began to hope.

Davies' condition deteriorated on the steep parts of the track down towards the high ledge. At some points they were forced to stop and help the private down places he couldn't negotiate and Banks saw there was fresh blood showing at the wounded ankle. By the time they reached the ledge Davies could hardly put any weight on that foot.

"I need to bind it again, Cap," he said. "That, and a wee shot of morphine should see me ready for another stretch."

While Wilkins gave Davies a hand with dressing the wound, Banks and Wiggo walked to the other end of the ledge and looked at the trail that went down the slope.

"Yon's more of a climb than a walk," the sergeant said.

"Aye. The lad will never make it that way. And it's too narrow for us to be carrying him down it."

"Do we have an alternative?"

"We do. But you're not going to like it. We go back into the temple, back down the stairs, and out the main door the way we came in."

"Past all them beasties? We'd never make it. We don't have enough firepower left."

"Not if they're still there, I agree. But if our luck's in, they're all away up top feeding on the mess we left earlier."

"Be fair, Cap. When has our luck ever been in?"

"We've got to chance it, for the lad's sake if nothing else."

"Let me go through first for a shufti then."

"No, there'll be no splitting up; that's what got us into trouble in the first place. We all go through. You bring up the rear. And keep an eye on Davies.

He's a tough lad. But he's in trouble."

Banks was first into the narrow crevasse. It was as tight a squeeze as he remembered from the day before but the fact that he knew he'd made it through the last time made it somehow easier and it was less than a minute before he emerged at the top of the stairs high above the temple floor. The area below lay in shadow but there was no sound of the beetles' high drone, no odor to indicate their presence. As soon as the others had come through to join him, he took to the stairs, descending slowly and quietly.

The farther down they went the more it became apparent that the temple was empty of the beasts; more than that, it was empty of all remnants of the ones the squad had left dead in their wake their last time through here. The bodies of the researchers and the Victorian squad were still laid out in rows, and if it wasn't for the toppled and smashed idol that lay amid them, Banks might have been wondering if their last time here hadn't been some kind of fever dream.

They reached the temple floor with no mishap. Davies' injury was still slowing him down but he was taking the stairs with only a hint of a limp; Banks guessed the morphine might be having something to do with that.

Wilkins looked at the bodies of the researchers. Two of them were buried beneath large chunks of the fallen idol, only their legs showing.

"We can't leave them like this," he said.

"We can't take them with us, and we don't have

time to bury them. Besides, if we move them, we might alert the beasts to the fact we're here."

"That's ascribing a lot of intelligence to them, Cap."

"Given what we've seen so far, I'm not sure I'm ascribing enough." He looked down at the dead. "We'll see that their families get told. That's all we can do for them now."

Without a look back he made for the main entranceway. With the squad at his back he stepped through and looked over the plain. He'd been right; he'd underestimated the beasts' intelligence.

The plain was covered in a horde of the beasts in sizes from small dog to almost elephantine. Every one of them was up on their legs and all heads were turned on the entrance way, focussed on the squad.

The high drone started up out on the open area and was answered from higher up in the city by a chorus that sounded like an army on the march. On looking back through the doorway he saw the concourse beyond already filling with more of the beasts and, behind that, a darker area that resolved into a view of the house-sized thing they'd seen in the crater coming down through the city with the other beasts swarming around it as if in supplication.

They were caught in the open with no escape route.

The beetles began to advance.

-DAVIES-

"Back to back," the captain said, "for all the good it's going to do us. Let's take as many of these fuckers with us as we can."

Davies happened to be the one facing the main gate when they formed up and so was first to see the beasts there move aside and the big one make its way forward. It moved slowly, majestically Davies thought, as if it knew it was king of all it surveyed here in this place. It raised a black pincer the size of a horse as if waving to its subjects in acknowledgement. All other movement on the plain stopped as the beetle reached the doorway. It filled the whole arch, almost as if the gate had been made for the purpose.

"Fucking hell," Wiggo said, "it's built like a fucking tank."

"Well that's handy," the captain said. "It so happens we've got a way of dealing with tanks. Quick, lads. Grenades, before it gets out of the gate."

All four of them took a grenade each.

"On three, pull the pins. Don't throw them high. Lob them under it, take it out from below. One, two...three."

Following Banks' lead, they lobbed the grenades underhand just above ground level. The beast caught one of them with a great pincer, the other three rolled out of sight below it, and the squad had just enough time to throw themselves to the ground before the grenades went up with a crack that echoed around the canyon.

Banks got them on their feet as soon as the roar faded, weapons raised. The huge beetle lay in the doorway, a great seeping hole all along the back of its shell, its head totally vaporized and smoking. Its bulk blocked the main entry to the city; none of the beasts backed up behind it would be able to get over it, for a few seconds at least. A high drone rose from all the beasts on this side of the gateway but now it didn't seem coordinated, as if some kind of coherence had been lost. Davies' suspicion was proved right when he looked over the plain; the beasts were no longer paying attention to the squad. Some were already heading to the fallen creature in the gateway to scavenge its parts, others, more than half of them, had taken to fighting among themselves. The plain became a battleground of snapping pincers and flying black ichor.

"Leg it, lads," Banks shouted. "To the cliff, before they get round to electing a new leader."

Davies was slow to push off on his bad foot and the others were already three paces ahead before he even got going but that proved to be a blessing in disguise for the three of them provided an arrowhead wedge with the captain in front and Wiggo and Wilkins on either side. Davies was able to slot into the space behind them and gain a degree of protection while they dodged fighting beetles, snapping pincers and pools of tarry goop. So far none of them had needed to use their weapons; the beetles were more concerned with fighting each other. As if to prove the point, two of the beasts took down a large one only five yards to the squad's left as they ran past. That was a cue for a swarm to pour over the dead one. It was already in pieces before Davies passed it.

Davies tried to concentrate on the captain's back, one step at a time, trying to ignore the pain. He felt wetness and heat at his ankle again, more blood flowing into his boot. The flight to get off the valley floor turned into a prolonged feat of endurance as white flaring agony shot up his leg and his limp got ever more pronounced.

They were halfway to the cliff path before they had to fire their first shots; one of the larger beetles took an interest in them and headed in from their right flank. Davies took out its front legs. Wiggo heard the shots, turned and fired, blowing its head apart and within seconds the spot where it fell was a mound of swarming, snapping, feeding.

We're going to make it.

The captain reached the cliff path first and headed down, the others at his back. Davies chanced one last look back at the carnage that was still playing out before the great wall. The beetles' fighting was now concentrated around a series of seething mounds of frenzied feeding. Over at the main gate was another, even larger mound where the beetle king was being scavenged for parts. A cacophony of drones and whistles echoed around the canyon walls but almost as soon as Davies began on the downward trail the noise got softer, less insistent and soon it was drowned out by the pounding of blood in his ears. His senses narrowed, his sight concentrating on where he put his feet, everything else subsumed by the agony that shot through his body with every step. His mind played tricks on him; one minute he was on a high trail on a mountainside looking over desert sands, the next he was fleeing down a graffiti laden stairwell in a Glasgow tower block, screaming tormentors at his heels.

"Give us a smile, blackie, so we can see where you are."

He realised he had a rifle in his hands at the same instant as he heard heavy footfalls only a pace or two behind him. He screamed, years of pent-up fury unleashed as he swivelled on his bad foot, letting the pain guide him rather than take him.

"Come and get me if you think you've got the balls for it."

He didn't need to aim; the dark shape loomed up right there at the end of his barrel. He fired at it until it went away. The recoil took his balance, his pack decided its weight was better off going backwards and Davies tumbled down the rocky path, arse over tit. His bad ankle hit a jutting rock, white pain became cold dark and he fell gratefully into it.

He came out of it lying on his back looking up at a carpet of stars. A dark shape loomed at his left and he reached for a weapon, any weapon but stopped when he heard Wiggo's laugh.

"Look who's in the land of the living. Welcome

back, lad."

Davies tried to sit up. Pain shot through him at both ends, white hot in his ankle, red hot and sticky at the back of his head when he felt there.

"You took a wee bump. Well, a big bump really. But no worries; we're back at yon oasis and we're safe and away. We lugged you here like a sack of coal. The beasties gave up the chase after you took out yon last one on the path and we've even got you a ride the rest of the way back."

"I took out one on the path? I thought that was just a dream."

"Well if this is one of your dreams, it's got me in it, you fucking pervert."

Off to his left, a camel, the same one as they'd met on the way in, brayed in answering laughter.

-BANKS-

The end of the story came a week later. Banks joined the rest of the squad in the mess in Lossiemouth. Wiggo and Wilkins stood, Davies didn't; the private had his left leg in a cast up to his knee and had it resting straight out on a spare chair.

After standing for a round of beers, Banks produced some notes from his pocket.

"Two things to tell you that I learned from the colonel in my debrief.

"Firstly, there's been a wee volcano eruption in a remote part of Libya. A research team from Edinburgh was unfortunately caught up in it and there were no survivors. Their families have been notified. Off the record, the Libyan Air Force did a bit of target practice at our suggestion. Yon crater, city, and everything around it, is now a pile of rubble.

"Secondly, and more happily, they've traced the mannie who wrote the journal back then. He was never done for shooting his C.O., and I might have left that bit out of my report to the colonel. He stayed in service for years after walking out of the desert, won a wheen of medals, retired to a wee house in the Highlands and died in his bed with his family around him at the age of ninety. We would all do well to be so lucky."

Banks raised his glass.

"To squads, old and new."

They drank some beer.

Then they drank some more.

 SEVERED**PRESS**

🐦 @severedpress
f /severedpress

Check out other great
Cryptid Novels!

J.H. Moncrieff
RETURN TO DYATLOV PASS

In 1959, nine Russian students set off on a skiing expedition in the Ural Mountains. Their mutilated bodies were discovered weeks later. Their bizarre and unexplained deaths are one of the most enduring true mysteries of our time. Nearly sixty years later, podcast host Nat McPherson ventures into the same mountains with her team, determined to finally solve the mystery of the Dyatlov Pass incident. Her plans are thwarted on the first night, when two trackers from her group are brutally slaughtered. The team's guide, a superstitious man from a neighboring village, blames the killings on yetis, but no one believes him. As members of Nat's team die one by one, she must figure out if there's a murderer in their midst—or something even worse—before history repeats itself and her group becomes another casualty of the infamous Dead Mountain.

Gerry Griffiths
CRYPTID ZOO

As a child, rare and unusual animals, especially cryptid creatures, always fascinated Carter Wilde. Now that he's an eccentric billionaire and runs the largest conglomerate of high-tech companies all over the world, he can finally achieve his wildest dream of building the most incredible theme park ever conceived on the planet... CRYPTID ZOO. Even though there have been apparent problems with the project, Wilde still decides to send some of his marketing employees and their families on a forced vacation to assess the theme park in preparation for Opening Day. Nick Wells and his family are some of those chosen and are about to embark on what will become the most terror-filled weekend of their lives—praying they survive. STEP RIGHT UP AND GET YOUR FREE PASS... TO CRYPTID ZOO

SEVERED**PRESS**

🐦 @severedpress
f /severedpress

Check out other great
Cryptid Novels!

Edward J. McFadden III

THE CRYPTID CLUB

When cryptozoologist Ash Cohn receives a gold embossed printed invitation inviting him to join The Cryptid Club, he sees the resolution to all his problems.Famous cryptid scientist and biologist, Lester Treemont, one of the world's richest men, and the leader of the Cryptid Club, is dying. What he offers via his invitation is a chance to succeed him. To take over his wealth, laboratory, and discoveries. All Ash has to do is beat eight others like him in a series of tests both mental and physical involving Treemont's collection of cryptids. Seems simple enough, and Ash has nothing to lose.Nine strangers from across the globe, all with reasons for wanting to win. When they start dying one by one, the competition shifts to one of survival. Who among them will rise to the top and reign over The Cryptid Club?

William Meikle

INFESTATION

It was supposed to be a simple mission. A suspected Russian spy boat is in trouble in Canadian waters. Investigate and report are the orders. But when Captain John Banks and his squad arrive, it is to find an empty vessel, and a scene of bloody mayhem. Soon they are in a fight for their lives, for there are things in the icy seas off Baffin Island, scuttling, hungry things with a taste for human flesh. They are swarming. And they are growing. "Scotland's best Horror writer" - Ginger Nuts of Horror "The premier storyteller of our time." - Famous Monsters of Filmland

Check out other great

Cryptid Novels!

Hunter Shea

THE DOVER DEMON

The Dover Demon is real...and it has returned. In 1977, Sam Brogna and his friends came upon a terrifying, alien creature on a deserted country road. What they witnessed was so bizarre, so chilling, they swore their silence. But their lives were changed forever. Decades later, the town of Dover has been hit by a massive blizzard. Sam's son, Nicky, is drawn to search for the infamous cryptid, only to disappear into the bowels of a secret underground lair. The Dover Demon is far deadlier than anyone could have believed. And there are many of them. Can Sam and his reunited friends rescue Nicky and battle a race of creatures so powerful, so sinister, that history itself has been shaped by their secretive presence? "THE DOVER DEMON is Shea's most delightful and insidiously terrifying monster yet." – Shotgun Logic Reviews "An excellent horror novel and a strong standout in the UFO and cryptid subgenres." –Hellnotes "Non-stop action awaits those brave enough to dive into the small town of Dover, and if you're lucky, you won't see the Demon himself!" – The Scary Reviews PRAISE FOR SWAMP MONSTER MASSACRE "B-horror movie fans rejoice, Hunter Shea is here to bring you the ultimate tale of terror!" – Horror Novel Reviews "A nonstop thrill ride! I couldn't put this book down." – Cedar Hollow Horror Reviews

Armand Rosamilia

THE BEAST

The end of summer, 1986. With only a few days left until the new school year, twins Jeremy and Jack Schaffer are on very different paths. Jeremy is the geek, playing Dungeons & Dragons with friends Kathleen and Randy, while Jack is the jock, getting into trouble with his buddies. And then everything changes when neighbor Mister Higgins is killed by a wild animal in his yard. Was it a bear? There's something big lurking in the woods behind their New Jersey home. Will the police be able to solve the murder before more Middletown residents are ripped apart?

Printed in Great Britain
by Amazon

65833646R00078